Into the Paracosm

Tixa Carvalho

Cover design and Illustration by Sónia Correia
soniacorreia1998@gmail.com

ISBN: 978-989-33-6770-4

First Edition

CHAPTER 1

THE NIGHT WIND carries the putrid stench of decay, something you wouldn't expect from the wealthiest part of St. Marrow. The rain stopped, but water still drips from the old pipes.

Litter and debris crunch beneath Violet's boots, her footsteps muffled among rowdy casinos and drunken bar fights. She throws an occasional glance over her shoulder, failing to notice a person in her path.

"Watch it, blondie," the man growls, part of his drink spilling on the floor.

"Oh, sorry about that," Violet smirks, stepping aside. "I must have missed your *Do Not Disturb* sign."

"You little—"

As the big clock strikes midnight, the curfew alarm erupts from the speakers with a deafening roar. Its sound resonates as a turbulent blend of a rough scream and a piercing shriek. Infuriating as it may be, there's no denying its effectiveness.

Fear replaces anger in the man's eyes. With a muttered curse, he hurriedly retreats, disappearing into the maze of darkened streets.

BANG!

Violet crouches, covering her ears. She bites back the gasp that swells at the back of her throat. Instinct forces her to reach for her calf, ready to wield her knife.

Her mind races. Guards appear in the distance—flashlight in one hand, gun in the other. They're getting ready to roam the streets.

Shit.

I need to get out of here.

Violet dashes through a narrow alley, clutching a brown paper package to her chest, running as fast and as long as her legs can carry her. The city's decaying buildings loom above her, casting long shadows that seem to mock her every move. Beads of sweat form on her temple, free flowing until they drip from her chin. Filthy air burns her throat as she inhales deeper, faster. With one swift movement she pulls up her face mask, covering her mouth and nose.

Her arm throbs with a sharp pain as a broken glass shard protruding from a crumbling wall grazes her skin. She winces, biting her lip to stifle a cry, but quickly pushes the pain aside.

Violet approaches the rendezvous point. From the outside, it appears to be nothing but an old factory—because it is. An abandoned and weathered down factory concealed within the forgotten corners of the city. Its cracked walls and shattered windows allow nature to reclaim it in a tangle of overgrown weeds and vines. As she enters, the creaking door protests her intrusion, a sound that has become all too familiar.

The air hangs heavy with deterioration, blending seamlessly with the city. She navigates the dim corridors, cautious steps over rotting oak floors. A broken light bulb flickers, casting eerie shadows on peeling walls.

I hate this place.

She relies on muscle memory, each floorboard guiding her through the darkness. Violet turns right, guided by intuition. She maneuvers through rubble with ease. The wind stirs forgotten papers, adding a ghostly touch. Distant dripping water and a faint hum shatter the prevailing silence.

I'm close.

An aged wooden door with a faint glimmer of light seeping through the keyhole invites her to Dr. Parcel's office. Two guards stand on each side, stance firm but their faces emotionless.

Violet ignores them, and knocks.

"Obey the Council." A rough, deep voice says.

"I've got your package," she responds, holding it up.

"Obey the Council."

"Seriously?"

She knocks again. Once, twice and then a third time. A chuckle emanates from the other side, accompanied by the heavy thud of approaching footsteps.

"Obey the Council."

Violet rolls her eyes. "Survive the fog."

As Dr. Parcel swings open the door, his gaze fixates on her, scrutinizing every inch. His secret office exudes an authoritarian energy that Violet has always hated. Stacks of untouched books and piles of abandoned files draped in cobwebs and dust sit as remnants of negligence and disuse.

"You're late," he growls, waddling back to his seat. "You're getting slower."

She clenches her teeth, meeting his remark head on. Her eyes narrow as they trail down to the struggling legs of the tiny chair beneath him.

"And you're getting bigger," she retorts, muttering between her teeth.

Taking a seat across from him, Violet rests her black boots on his table. From the depths of her jacket, she retrieves the package, tossing it towards Dr. Parcel.

Dr. Parcel's eyes scan the package, his gaze fixating on a scratch across its exterior. A crease forms between his eyebrows. "What's this?" he grumbles, lifting it to his nose and inhaling deeply. A faint smirk tugs at his lips. "It smells like someone will only be receiving half the payment."

Violet's eyes widen, shifting between him and the package. "Dr. Parcel," she begins, attempting to steady her voice, "please take a closer look. The scratch is merely superficial; otherwise, all the pills would be spilling out."

He settles back into his chair, intertwining his fingers atop his belly. "We cannot afford this to be a recurring issue. I am putting my position and my reputation in the High Council at risk by hiring rats like you, so I demand flawless execution."

She straightens her back, her shoulders squared, and locks eyes with Dr. Parcel. Her gaze is steady, but her fingers twist at her sides. "I know. I understand the stakes. It won't happen again." She swallows her own saliva along with her pride.

Dr. Parcel, his large frame spilling over the edges of his chair, remains unmoved. With a grunt, he drops the package onto the floor. He leans forward, his sausage-like finger jutting out and pointing directly at her. "It won't happen again," he says, his voice clipped and unyielding, "Because I won't be hiring you."

Violet's hands slam down on the table, the impact making the surface tremble. Her eyes widen in a mix of disgust and fear, her breath quickening. "That's not fair," she says, her voice rising in pitch, cracking with strain. "I've risked my life. I've been working so hard and—"

"One more word out of that filthy mouth and you're not getting a single coin from me, rat." Violet's jaw tightens, her teeth grinding together as she forces herself to sit back down. Her fingers dig into the edge of the chair, knuckles white. "Consider yourself lucky I'm even paying for a job poorly executed."

Dr. Parcel reaches into a drawer, retrieving a crumpled wad of cash. He tosses it onto the table, the bills scattering haphazardly across the surface.

Violet reaches out and snatches the money, her fingers grazing each note as she gathers them in her hand. Clenching her fist tightly around the cash, she forces herself to count it.

One... two... three... Violet's mind tallies the value, her eyes narrowing with each addition. The sum won't cover even half of what she needs. She tucks the money into a hidden pocket, ensuring it remains secure. She looks down at the table, defeated. She squeezes her own kneecaps with firm hands to keep herself from trembling.

With a grunt, Dr. Parcel musters the strength to rise from the chair, its legs creaking back into place. "Well, it's time for me to—"

"Parcel."

"Doctor," he corrects curtly.

"Dr. Parcel. Do you have any more jobs for me?"

He shakes his head, his expression twisting into a sneer. "I don't have anything for you. In fact, I'd suggest you find somewhere else to waste your time. If you linger here any longer, you might start costing me more than you're worth."

Dr. Parcel makes a show of turning his back, his movements deliberate and disdainful. He grabs a coat from the back of his chair and throws it over his shoulder. "Now get out. I have no use for the failures of your kind."

Violet scrambles to her feet, her hands feeling for the wad of cash inside her pocket as if making sure it's still there. Without a word, she hurries towards the door.

She pushes through the factory's decaying corridors, each step heavier than the one before. The sound of Dr. Parcel locking the door behind her echoing in her head.

The air in the factory feels colder now. It's claustrophobic—as if the walls are closing in on her. She passes the broken window where a few stray beams of moonlight penetrate the grime-coated glass, their weak glow making the factory's neglect even more apparent. Her shoulders slump forward, her head hanging low, the weight of her failure bearing down on her.

As she exits the factory, she pauses on the threshold, her fingers gripping the door frame, gaze fixed on the darkened alleyway ahead.

The tall clock tower is still visible, bold black numbers signing two hours past curfew. It's too dangerous to stay here. She can't go back to the forest either. It would take her at least an hour to get back to the cabin. If assassins and robbers don't get her, the wild animals definitely will. The village is her only option.

The back exit of the factory leads to the barrier. A tall brick wall contours noble territory. It rises from the earth tall and strong. No visible cracks. No moss or vines growing in between. Tax payers, wealthy families, and government workers stay in, everyone else out.

A perfectionist's work—except for thirty loose bricks next to the sewers.

Violet removes brick by brick, placing them in soft grass. It creates an opening—a secret passage. Guards are too preoccupied with gates and stone arches. No one bothers patrolling abandoned buildings after curfew.

She crawls through the opening, closing the gap right after. It doesn't matter that it's the thousandth time she's using the hidden passage. Every time feels like the first. Every movement, every sound, every flicker of light resembles death coming for her. Her movements are erratic, her hands shaking. She struggles to breathe as if the air itself is strangling her.

Dark concrete fades into dirt roads as soon as Violet steps out of the city walls. To the left, a path full of trees and danger signs leading up to the forest. To the right, a path of misery.

Sadness seeps into the cracks of the worn sidewalk and stretches across the empty fields. This path, once familiar, feels even sadder during winter nights. Memories flood in, back to the time before the division of the city, before the fog.

Stores that were once loaded with designer goods are either closed, in ruins or moved somewhere else. Frail tents have replaced the restaurants where she used to dine with her parents, now serving as the makeshift trading posts for farmers during the day.

Proud workers turned into cockroaches of society. Farmers, and numerous unfortunate families of commoners are now reduced to empty eyes and unamused faces, stripped of hope. The villages near the fog surrounding St. Marrow have been utterly neglected by the High Council.

"It's for the children," people said as they departed, justifying their choice. "We can't risk our kids wandering into the fog, falling prey to the monsters," they reasoned.

The monsters.

Shadow figures, described in countless ways, inhabit the fog that has surrounded St. Marrow for over a century. At first, people were skeptical, dismissing them as hoaxes, pranks, or mere urban legends—but they are real. With numerous deaths and disappearances, people stopped trying to leave. Survivors returned, marked by their encounters, sharing their stories as a warning. The monsters are no longer a myth.

Violet knows their reality all too well. Her parents had promised her freedom from this city on her fifteenth birthday, meticulously preparing for their escape. Her father, a devoted cop, ventured ahead to ensure a safe path. Her mother was lured in by his screams, his panic—his pleas for help. So, they took her next. Violet was left behind five years ago, scarred by the echoes of her mother's cries and her father's desperate struggle.

Nostalgia fades from Violet's mind as the biting winter cold seeps into her bones, exacerbating the discomfort of her injured arm. She exhales onto her hands for warmth, but the night air steals heat faster than her body can replace it.

Her gaze shifts to the houses that line the village. Constructed haphazardly, the houses stand as a patchwork of salvaged materials and makeshift solutions. Ramshackle walls, weathered and crumbling. Roofs of corrugated metal sheets sag under the weight of discarded debris, revealing gaps that allow the freezing wind to whistle through.

The structures seem to lean on each other for support as wooden planks, worn and splintered, act as makeshift walkways between the homes, bridging the gaps between the muddy ground and the thresholds.

The silence of the night is broken only by the occasional sound of a creaking door or a distant cough.

Violet stops in her tracks when she reaches a house with a chalk mural on its side. The creation, a charming masterpiece crafted by the hands of children, depicts a delightful scene—a sun, a tree, and a house—splashed in a limited yet vivid selection of colors.

This is it.

She knocks on the door, quiet enough not to cause a commotion, but strong enough to be heard. The curtains flutter. Footsteps approach the door, and as it creaks open, a voice tinged with both surprise and relief utters her name.

"Violet?"

Violet musters a weak yet genuine smile, her exhaustion momentarily concealed by the comfort of familiarity. "Hi Ingrid. Can I come in?" She tugs at the sleeve of her jacket, revealing her injury.

Ingrid's eyes widen, a gasp escaping her lips as she instinctively brings her wrinkled hands to cover her mouth. She wastes no time, guiding Violet into the refuge of her home, firmly shutting the door behind them.

She guides Violet without uttering a word, leading her to a cozy corner of her cold home, where a comfortable armchair awaits. A kind smile graces Ingrid's face as she retrieves a small wooden box from under a few scattered blankets.

"Open it, dear," Ingrid gently urges, placing the box in Violet's hands.

Violet lifts the lid, revealing an array of ointments and bandages, each bearing the marks of use and care. It's the same collection she has seen Ingrid use countless times whenever the children in the neighborhood would stumble and scrape their knees while playing outdoors.

She helps Violet remove her jacket; her hands shaky yet gentle. Her tired eyes assess the injury—a clean cut, a fortunate turn of events considering the size of the glass shard. Surprise flickers across Ingrid's face as Violet retrieves the crumpled money from an inside pocket of her jacket.

"It's not much," Violet whispers, hints of concern in her voice, "but I promise I'll bring more. Please, send Ethan inside the barrier tomorrow. Use this to secure food for the children and yourselves. And if there are any injured in need of medicine, get it for them too."

Ingrid takes the money from Violet's hands and sets it aside, placing a small rock on top to guard it against the whispers of wind that creep through the worn crevices of their shelter. Not a word passes between them until she starts cleaning and dressing the wound, her hands moving with practiced precision.

"What happened this time?" Ingrid asks.

Violet's gaze falls, a veil of shame casting over her features. "I... I fell," she murmurs, words bringing a bitter taste to her mouth as she lies.

Ingrid clicks her tongue softly, yet she chooses not to pry further.

"You know," Ingrid begins, her voice quiet and raspy, "Stephanie's father is seeking someone to assist him in gathering firewood. He offers not just food, but also a room. It may not be much, but you'd be sheltered and safe at all times."

Violet knows this speech too well. The villagers, all of them, urging her to abandon her ventures inside the barrier, to find a modest job that provides just enough sustenance. They are well-intentioned, but wrong. If she were to heed their advice, who would find the means to nourish all the hungry mouths and care for all the sick bodies? The community had been withering away before Violet secured her spot within Dr. Parcel's schemes. Now, they're at least surviving.

Guilt gnaws at Violet as she watches the financial lifeline she'd hoped to secure now shattered. The realization stings sharply, making her question how things might have unfolded differently had she been more diligent, more precise, or simply more capable. The weight of her inadequacy presses heavily on her chest.

A lump forms in her throat as the harsh truth becomes undeniable: she has no choice but to return to a life of theft and smuggling. The thought of slipping back into the shadows of the city, scraping together what she can from the dark underbelly of St. Marrow, settles over her like as heavy as the fog. Despite her best efforts, no amount of pilfered goods or stolen supplies can replace the stability and security that money once promised.

With the wound now tended to, Violet reaches out, gently squeezing Ingrid's hand. "Thank you," she murmurs, her voice trembling slightly. "You and the children are more than family to me. I would do anything to ensure your safety."

As the heartfelt moment unfolds, a door swings open with a jolt, startling both of them.

"Ethan?" Violet's eyes widen.

"Violet?" Ethan exclaims, his voice filled with a mix of surprise and concern. "I knew it. Thought I heard your voice." His expression turns serious, overriding the warmth of their reunion. "Sorry to interrupt, grandma," he says urgently. "But Rosie's fever is back, and it's getting worse. I need your help."

A flicker of worry and sadness passes over Ingrid's face as she struggles to rise from her seat. "I'll be right there," she reassures him before turning back to Violet. "I'll be back with you, dear."

Ingrid leaves the room, leaving behind a lingering blend of awkwardness and tension.

With the weight of the interrupted moment still palpable, Violet hesitates before breaking the silence. "Your daughter is sick?" she asks.

Ethan takes a seat where his grandma was previously sitting, his gaze fixed on the floor. "She's been feverish the past few days," he confides, his voice tinged with worry. "It's been tough."

"I see." Violet looks down into her own intertwined fingers. "I hope she gets better soon."

A heavy, suffocating quiet descends upon the room, stretching the seconds into what feels like eternal hours.

"Violet," Ethan stammers. She lifts her gaze, meeting his eyes for a fleeting moment. "Are you spending the night?"

"I'll have the couch if it's ok with Ingrid, but I'm leaving before sunrise."

"I'll get you some more blankets." Ethan says as he leaves, following his grandma to the children's room.

No amount of experience could ease Violet's discomfort with going back to stealing. She's a thief—a *rat*. She braces herself for the return to a life she had hoped to escape, aware that her struggle for survival is far from over.

I'm not ready.

She forces herself to stand and shuffles to the couch, covering her chest with an extra pillow.

I don't want to be ready.

The wind howls outside. Violet's eyelids feel heavy. She craves coffee—a familiar comfort from Ingrid's kitchen. But she hesitates. Caffeine would only make her jittery and unstable. Jittery and unstable don't go well with handling a knife, but neither do tired and sleepless. She needs to be sharp for tomorrow's scavenging: more food, more medicine, more everything.

I'm just going to rest my eyes.
Five minutes.

CHAPTER 2

VIOLET RACES THROUGH the streets of St. Marrow, her heart pounding in rhythm with her steps. The curfew alarm echoed through the city two hours ago, pushing patrol guards to the far reaches, creating a brief window of opportunity.

The night workers begin their sluggish march to the factories, their faces drowning with fatigue. She slows her pace, blending in with the shadows. She pulls up her face mask, concealing her identity from the watchful eyes of the cameras that dot the area. All she needs is a small distraction—a truck left unattended, something, anything.

A supply truck rumbles into view, its heavy wheels grinding against the uneven cobblestones. Violet trails the driver, staying just out of sight. The truck halts behind a ration center, its engine idling. The driver, a burly man with a grizzled beard, hauls supply boxes into a narrow alleyway.

She edges closer, crouching behind a dark doorway.

"The quality control delays from Parcel are unacceptable."

A voice that sends a shiver down her spine. Violet peeks out, just enough to take a look at him before retreating back to her hiding place.

"We need those shipments on time, or it's our necks on the line," he snaps. "Get Parcel on the phone. Now."

Lucius Creed, a High Council member—Minister of commerce and trade—stands amidst the workers. Eyes jet-black, holding a fearsome and intimidating gaze. His jaw, sharp as a blade, clenches.

"Parcel's become utterly unreliable," Creed says. A murmur of agreement ripples through the workers. He continues, his voice lowering but still audible. "And these village rats," he sneers, "they're getting sicker and sicker. Farm productivity is plummeting. Such a major inconvenience."

Violet listens, her eyes narrowing. Her vision blurs and she can only see red. Her fingers twitch in anticipation. She becomes more and more aware of the knife strapped to her leg. It takes every inch of self-control in her body not to use it.

Creed's heartless words slice through the night air, each syllable a testament to his disregard for human life. To him, people are mere resources to be shuffled and discarded, problems to be managed. This man embodies everything wrong with the High Council. Everything wrong with St. Marrow—his cold indifference to the villagers, to their suffering; his irritation at the smallest disruption to his precious trade.

A worker, eyes darting nervously around, steps hesitantly towards Creed. His face pales as he approaches.

"Sir," he says, voice trembling, "we're still trying to reach Dr. Parcel, but he's not –"

Creed's expression darkens instantly. His fingers tighten around the edges of the paperwork he's holding as he exhales sharply. "Forget it," he interrupts, his voice cold and cutting. "I'll just sign these papers myself."

Creed strides towards the entrance of the building. The worker nods quickly, his relief tangible as he hurries to follow the imposing figure.

A worker glances back at the boxes stacked haphazardly in the alleyway. "What about these?"

"Nothing to worry about," another one scoffs, adjusting his cap. "With the curfew in place, no one will even dare come near."

Wait.

"Indeed," a third worker agrees, waving his hand dismissively. "The curfew keeps the vermin away. Let's finish this and get out of here."

Wait…

All of them follow Creed inside, door slamming shut behind them with a resonant thud. The alleyway falls into silence, the only sound the faint rustle of the night breeze and the occasional drip from a leaky pipe.

Now!

The sound of footsteps receding is her cue. She darts towards the nearest box, her movements quick yet silent. With a desperate shove, she pries it open, the lid groaning as it gives way.

Her eyes widen as the contents are revealed—jackpot. The box is stuffed with meal bars, stacked high and ready to be devoured. The posh version of a protein bar. Nutritious and easy to transport, as the flyers boast.

Violet's heart races with a mix of relief and urgency. She stuffs her pockets with bars, her movements frantic and erratic. She shoves handfuls of them into her jacket, the bulging fabric of the pockets straining under the weight. Her hands tremble, and in her haste, several bars slip from her grasp, hitting the ground with muffled thuds.

The sound resonances through the alley, each thud louder than the last. Violet freezes.

She scans for movement. There is none.

The sound of rustling fabric and quick footsteps echoes in the darkness.

Shit.

Her movements become quick and sharp—collecting the fallen meal bars and stuffing them back into her pockets. She bolts towards the end of the alley. Her breath comes in ragged gasps, her pulse pounding in her ears.

Her left foot slips on the wet concrete as she rounds the first corner, just as the guards burst into view from the opposite end of the alley.

"Stop!" One of them yells, but Violet's legs keep going.

"Over here!"

"Thief!"

Hide.

I need to hide.

Violet runs into the main street, right before the barrier's exit. She jumps into the nearest rainwater barrel. Cold water burns her skin and weighs down her clothes. She listens, holding her breath. The guards' footsteps grow louder, then fainter, as they rush past her hiding spot. She doesn't move until she hears nothing but the wind.

They're gone.

She pleads with her body for one final burst of strength to free her torso. She swings her right leg out first, making sure her foot is fully stable on the ground. She shivers, so much that she's unable to form a coherent thought for the first few seconds. She hugs her own body, desperate for heat as her lungs drink the air in noisy rasps.

She walks out of the barrier just far enough to escape the guards' view. She quickens her pace until she's behind a broken market stall. She sits, pressing her back against the splintered and rotting wood.

Violet pulls a bar from her pocket, the plastic crinkling under her fingers. The meal bars are safe, at least, their packaging keeping them dry. She clutches it close to her chest, taking deep breaths.

Worth it.

The road ahead is familiar but daunting. With each step towards the village, the air thickens. The closer to the fog, the harder to breathe. The further she goes, the stuffier it becomes, like a damp blanket pressing against her face.

Violet sees the village in the distance. Despite the cold night air biting at her soaked clothes, a warmth spreads through her chest. Her thoughts turn to Ingrid, the children, all the villagers, to their faces lighting up, realizing they won't go hungry tonight.

As she steps into the village, her heart sinks at the sight before her. The usual stillness of the late hour is shattered by the restless murmur of voices. She pushes through the gathering crowd, catching fragments of hushed conversations.

"Did you hear? They said the fever was so high, nothing could bring it down. How could this happen?"

"The fever's spreading, you know. We're all on edge, hoping our own children don't fall ill."

Fear and sorrow carve deep lines into the villagers' faces. Mothers clutch their children close, tears glistening on their cheeks. Men stand with clenched fists, eyes scanning the crowd.

"It was a baby."

"It was just a baby"

Violet's breath catches in her throat—a child has died from a high fever. Her heart tightens, and her mind flashes to Ethan's daughter.

Rosie.

She moves fast, her footsteps urgent against the cold, irregular ground. She dodges through the crowd as the houses seem to blur together as she hurries towards Ingrid's home.

In the distance, the door to the children's house stands wide open. A harsh beam of light spills onto the darkened street.

She slips inside without a moment's hesitation, her eyes adjusting to the dim light. Ingrid, Ethan, and a handful of the kids—most likely awoken by the commotion outside—are huddled together. They stare blankly, their faces illuminated by the flickering shadows cast by a single, swaying oil lamp. The toddlers, too young to understand, are distracted by bits of fabric and an empty tin, while the older children look around with wide, frightened eyes, picking up on the adults' tension.

Violet's gaze locks on Ethan. She approaches him, each step heavy, legs trembling. "Was it…?" She doesn't muster the courage to let out Rosie's name, as if saying it would make it true.

"No, not Rosie." Ethan's eyes meet hers, red-rimmed and weary. He shakes his head slowly. "… not yet." His voice falters, then shatters as he allows his tears to flow down his face.

Relief sweeps through Violet, a fleeting comfort tangled with a heavy thread of guilt. The death of a child remains a tragedy, regardless of whose child it is. "Who was it?" she asks, her voice thin and strained.

"The milkman's son," Ingrid says, "Poor little thing was barely two years old."

The news hits her like a punch to the gut. She glances at the meal bars stuffed in her pockets.

It's not enough.

It will never be enough.

Violet nods towards the kitchen, urging Ingrid to follow. Ingrid gently places a toddler onto the rug, where the child curls up, already too tired and weak to stay awake.

In the dimly lit space, Violet pulls the meal bars from her pockets, her fingers trembling. Her lips tremble as much as her hands as she mutters her thanks, placing the bars inside an empty bucket on top of the table.

Not enough.

"How many sick are we dealing with?" Violet asks.

Ingrid's eyes drift away, hollow and distant, the exhaustion and grief catching up to her after all these years. "We've lost count, dear."

Violet lets out a heavy sigh, feeling the weight of their situation settle over her. She closes her eyes for a moment, drawing in a deep breath, steadying herself. "Do you have any spare clothes?"

Ingrid nods and gestures to a small storage room. The room is cluttered, filled with an assortment of sweaters and pants, worn-out but clean. She gets dressed — the fabric rough against her skin. As she changes, the cold, damp clothes she removes fall to the floor with a sodden thud.

"I'll be back for these later," Violet says, more to herself than Ingrid.

She returns to the main room, walking past everyone, her gaze fixed on the floor. The air is thick with the wheezing of strained breaths and soft, persistent coughs. The sound of life withering away inside these walls — inside this village.

Violet steps outside without uttering a single word. The cold night wind cuts through her, but she welcomes it, hoping it will numb the pain.

She closes the door behind her with a soft click. The sound triggers a surge within her, and she breaks into a sprint. Her heart pounds in her head, adrenaline pushing her into a rhythm of speed and strength she never knew she had. Tears blur her vision, the cold night air stealing them away before they can slip down her cheeks.

Dread swells up in her gut as the sky begins to lighten. The sun will rise soon, and the curfew will end.

The barrier looms in the distance. Her knees threaten to give in. She's exhausted, starving, injured — her body morphing into a puddle of sweat. Ingrid, the children, the villagers, their faces flash through her mind. She sprints ahead, faster and faster.

She charges towards the barrier, pulling out the loose bricks with clumsy, frantic movements. She slips through the gap, not bothering to close it before sprinting straight to the abandoned factory.

Violet enters the factory, her breath rough and uneven. She takes her usual path, her steps careless. A floorboard gives way beneath her, trapping her leg in the hole. She crashes down, pain shooting through her leg. Gritting her teeth, she pulls herself free and limps towards Dr. Parcel's office.

Reaching the door, she pounds her fist against the weathered wood, ignoring the guards.

"Who's there?" Dr. Parcel's voice rumbles from the other side, his coughs punctuating his words.

"Let me in!" Violet demands.

"Get rid of the rat! I have no time for this." Dr. Parcel's voice rises in irritation.

She throws her weight against the door one last time before the guards close in. They grab her by the shoulders, their grip firm. She thrashes, her arms swinging, her legs kicking out in a desperate attempt to free herself.

"I don't have a face ID!" she yells, her voice breaking.

The guards' hold tightens. Violet squirms against their iron grip, her body twisting with every effort to break free. Her feet slam against the floor, her fists punching the air in every direction.

"Let me go! I don't have—" Her struggles grow more frantic. One guard's hand clamps over her mouth, but she bites down hard, forcing him to pull back with a grunt. "I don't have a face ID!"

"Hold!" Dr. Parcel's voice cuts through the chaos. The guards hesitate, their hands pausing mid-air. The door creaks open just enough for him to peer out. His gaze locks onto Violet, eyes narrowing. "Come in."

He pushes the door wider, his bulk squeezing through the narrow gap. The gun, crammed into his waistband, juts out awkwardly.

Dr. Parcel moves towards his chair, his heavy footsteps reverberating against the floor. Violet sinks into the seat across from him, a seat she had hoped to never go back to.

"I thought I told you to get out of my face."

Violet clears her throat. "I need a job," she demands, steadying her voice. Dr. Parcel snorts. "I'm useful. I've got no face ID. No records. No way for your High Council cameras to track me."

Dr. Parcel's eyes narrow. "That's impossible. The cameras—"

Violet yanks up her face mask from under her sweater, cutting him off. "—don't see me."

Dr. Parcel's skepticism breaks into a harsh laugh, his belly shaking as he coughs between breaths. "You think that's going to work? The cameras would have detected any anomaly."

"No," she says, pulling her mask down. "Not me. I was pronounced dead five years ago when my parents disappeared in the fog. I was still fifteen. My ID was never registered."

His laughter fades, replaced by a calculating look somewhere between surprise and excitement. "So, you want work?" he asks, wiping tears from his eyes.

"Yes. Give me something. Anything."

His demeanor shifts. A sly smile plays at the corner of his lips as he leans in closer. "Anything?" he repeats. She nods, her heart racing in anticipation. "Well," he teases, lowering his voice and drawing out his words, "there might be something."

Something rushes through Violet's veins, and she's unable to point out if it's hope or desperation. "I'll take it."

"It's no easy task," he opens a file cabinet, the only well-kept and locked thing in the room. "These are high-profile clients, individuals of great value with substantial wealth. You may be in over your head."

"No matter what it is, I'll do it."

Dr. Parcel's smirk widens. "Very well," he chuckles, a tinge of excitement creeping into his voice. "If you insist."

He retrieves a cigar from his pocket, delicately placing it at the corner of his mouth, unlit. His thick fingers glide over the rows of files, accompanied by a gentle hum. Finally, his hand comes to a rest on a specific file, and he taps it softly with his index finger.

Retrieving the folder, he rejoins Violet at the table. From the same pocket, he takes out a small lighter and brings it close to the cigar. He ignites the tip, causing a tiny flame to flicker to life. As he takes a deep drag, the glow intensifies, and wisps of smoke spiral from his mouth. He exhales, a cloud of smoke billowing towards Violet, enveloping her momentarily. She coughs.

This pig.

"Tell me, rat," he begins, "are you familiar with the Paracosm?" A chuckle escapes his lips, mingling with another puff of smoke that oozes from both his nose and mouth. "Of course you are." He continues to puff on the cigar, as if punctuating his words with smoke-filled pauses. "You know the drill. Random citizens. An enclosed space full of fog. The usual."

Violet's fist tightens, her knuckles losing all color as she does so. "It's disgusting."

A smirk curls on Dr. Parcel's lips, his expression oozing with a mixture of amusement and superiority. "We're trying to find someone capable of defeating the monsters, or at the very least, find a way to survive in the fog."

"There *is* no way." She grunts through gritted teeth. "You guys are letting your people die every year for your own amusement. It's all fun and games to the High Council."

"You're right. There is no way. That's precisely why we're relentlessly looking for one. So, before you pass judgment, perhaps consider the bigger picture. No one likes an ungrateful brat."

Violet rises abruptly, her fists crashing against the table's surface, causing her chair to topple backwards in the process. "Enough of your games, Parcel. Cut the bullshit. What's the job?"

He releases a short, hearty belly laugh, blending with the swirling smoke as he indulges in another drag from his cigar. He pushes the file towards her, opening it on the first page. On it stands a picture of a young man wearing a police academy uniform, seemingly in his early twenties. Conrad Ashford.

Dr. Parcel leans forward. "You see," he begins, "his parents have expressed a deep desire to secure their son's safe return, and they are willing to offer a substantial sum of money to anyone capable of accomplishing this feat." He flips through the pages. "Within this file, you will find all the information you could possibly need. Blueprints, security details, and a list of personnel involved."

"So… you're telling me that he—"

"He's one of the prototypes selected for the Paracosm," he confirms, his tone matter-of-fact. He stubs out his cigar and seals the file shut. "The parents don't really care how you do it, as long as he is back home safe and unharmed."

Violet's gaze sharpens as her eyes narrow. "Your guards would just go look for him until they find him and bring him back."

Dr. Parcel waves his hand in a dismissive manner. "That's not our concern. My role is to find someone capable of undertaking the mission of retrieving him. Your job is to ensure it is accomplished. What happens after is none of our business."

Violet's muscles tense. "And if I get caught?"

A twisted smile creeps across Dr. Parcel's face, a glimmer of sinister amusement in his eyes. "Good luck."

CHAPTER 3

VIOLET MOVES THROUGH Ingrid's house. The dawn's first light peeks through the holes of the curtains, casting a faint glow over the room. She holds her breath, listening for any sign that someone might be waking up. She places the money advance from Dr. Parcel on top of the table, weighing it down with the usual small rock.

Under an empty glass of water, she leaves a note.

"Use this for food and medicine. Keep fighting for all of us. I will do the same. – V"

She pauses, her eyes lingering on the note. A lump forms in her throat, but she swallows it down. With a final look around the room, she slips out of the house and into the early morning light. She closes the door, twisting the knob all the way to minimize noise, feeling the cool metal under her palm.

"Where are you going?"

Violet jumps back, startled. Her back hits the door, eyes widening as if they're about to pop. Her pulse quickens, and she can almost feel the blood draining from her face.

"Ethan! Good morning," Violet says, voice cracking. "Sorry, I'm in a rush so—"

"Where are you going?" he repeats. "You never leave during the day."

"I have a job to do." She forces the words out, her mouth going dry.

"We don't go inside the barrier during the Paracosm Ceremony."

"I know, but I—"

"Don't." Ethan moves closer, shaking his head. "I lost my wife. I might lose Rosie any day now. I don't want to lose my best friend too."

"It's not like they would kill me," she argues, her words burning in her tongue as if she's unsure how true they are.

"I wouldn't put it past them. They're already slowly killing the entire village." Ethan firms his hand on the door. "Either that or they'll arrest you and send you to the sewers. They'll make you work yourself to death down there."

"I'm sorry." It's all she manages to say. It's too late to change her mind now.

Ethan's eyes shine and Violet can't tell if they're glowing with the rays of sun peeking through the clouds or unshed tears. He reaches out, gripping her shoulders. "Just... be careful. Promise me."

Violet nods, scared of making promises she can't commit to. His grip loosens as she turns her back on him, and leaves.

I'll do my best.

Violet makes her way through the village, the familiarity of farmers leaving for their fields and villagers repairing their houses bringing her some peace and comfort before she leaves.

Reaching the barrier, she pauses, taking in the city. Outside of the curfew it's as if St. Marrow has a life of its own. Vibrant colors everywhere shining under the comforting rays of winter sun.

Market stalls line the streets, their colorful canopies a stark contrast to the drab, gray buildings that loom above. Vendors shout, advertising fresh produce, handmade goods, and trinkets. The air is filled with the mingling scents of fresh bread, roasting meat, and the tangy aroma of fruit.

People move in groups, their faces vibrant as they chatter and laugh. Children run through the streets, their giggles ringing out as they play games, darting between the adults.

The signs of disparity are still evident. Beggars line the streets, sitting in small groups at every entrance to the barrier. The wealthy, in their fine clothes and polished shoes, walk past them without a second glance.

Violet blends into the crowd, her eyes constantly scanning her surroundings. The houses grow larger and richer as she nears the center of the city. Grand mansions with intricately designed facades, lush gardens, and iron gates stand in contrast to the rundown shacks she's used to in the village.

The city center is a hive of activity. Expensive cars with bright colors and smoother streets. Shop windows display luxurious goods — silks, jewelry, and finely crafted furniture. Premium citizens stroll leisurely, their conversations filled with talk of business, fashion, and the latest social events.

Violet keeps her head down, her mask pulled up to shield her face from the cameras. The police academy looms ahead, a stark, imposing structure. Its tall, stone walls and watchtowers give it the appearance of a fortress. Her pulse quickens as she approaches. According to Dr. Parcel's file, the

Paracosm Ceremony is taking place inside. She has to find her target before he's transported to the van.

The academy grounds are crowded with officials, guards, and curious bystanders. Banners in red and gold flutter in the breeze, adorned with the insignia of the High Council. A stage made out of thick wood has been set up with seven empty chairs, a podium and a microphone. Rows of seats are filled with VIPs and guests. All other attendees stand, forming a crowd beyond the rows of chairs.

Violet slips through the hordes of people. She finds a spot at the edge, partially hidden behind a stone pillar, giving her a clear view of the stage without drawing attention to herself.

The chief of police, a tall man in uniform, steps forward to the podium. His presence commands silence, and the crowd falls into a hushed stillness. With a voice that resonates through the square, he begins, "People of St. Marrow, we gather today to honor the traditions that keep our city strong and safe. Obey the Council."

The crowd, like a well-rehearsed chorus, responds in unison, "Survive the fog."

A chill runs down Violet's spine at the chant. The chief continues, "Today, we initiate the yearly Paracosm Ceremony, where citizens have been randomly selected to serve the greater good." He gestures to the side of the stage, where the High Council members wait to be announced. "It is my honor to present the members of the High Council."

The crowd erupts into cheers and applause. Banners wave more vigorously, and the air is filled with a cacophony of celebratory shouts. Violet rolls her eyes.

Idiots.

Brainwashed idiots.

"Lucius Creed, Minister of Commerce and Trade." Creed ascends the three steps leading to the stage. His gaze cuts through the crowd with a sharp edge. Violet knows him well; The tailored suit he wears, the precise way he moves—

his control over St. Marrow's economic pulse. His role in managing trade and resources ensures that the flow of wealth enriches himself and his allies on the Council.

"Isabelle Lancaster, Ministress of Propaganda and Social Affairs." Isabelle goes up next. Her beauty stands out even amid the splendor of the ceremony. Her smile is poised and every gesture calculated, a masterclass in manipulation. She ensures that only the Council's version of the truth prevails. Violet eyes some of the VIPs applauding extra hard as she takes her seat.

"Malachi Moore, Minister of Security and Law Enforcement." Malachi ascends with a commanding presence. He maintains order through fear, enforcing the laws with ruthless precision. The creator of the sewers' working camp. The crowd applauds in a stiff, orderly manner as he moves towards his chair.

"Sophia Cardinal, the new head of the Ministry of Conspiracy and Espionage." Sophia moves with a silent grace, her eyes darting around as if she's cataloging every face in the crowd. She's the unseen hand that neutralizes hidden threats. To this day no one knows how she managed to climb up the ranks and become a member of the High Council so quickly.

"Lilith Prim, from the Ministry of Culture and Education." Lilith walks up with an air of superiority. She shapes young minds, ensuring that future generations will uphold the Council's ideology. Her influence is felt in every cultural event and educational program.

"Dr. Marcus Parcel, Minister of Health and Resources." Dr. Parcel is slow, stairs creaking beneath his weight. He keeps his eyes straight ahead, not acknowledging the people until he is seated. Once he is comfortable in his chair, he scans the crowd, his gaze briefly brushing over Violet out of the corner of his eye.

The chief's voice falters as he continues, "And now, to introduce our new Minister of—" He pauses, scanning the side and back of the stage. "Minister of Infrastructure and Comfort, Benedict Laggard."

Lilith turns to Sophia. "He was right behind us."

Sophia nods. "Something's not right."

The stage remains empty where Benedict should be. The chief's brow furrows, confusion spreading among the citizens. He calls out again, louder, "Benedict Laggard?"

Whispers ripple through the crowd. People exchange bewildered glances. The noise escalates.

"Is he late?"

"Maybe he's missing."

"Does that mean we get to go home early?"

The chief's face turns a dark shade of red. "Quiet!" His voice rises but it's barely audible over the growing chaos. "Quiet, I said!" The commotion grows louder.

Violet's heart pounds. She watches as the chief of police exchanges tense glances with the other Council members. Sophia's eyes narrow, and Malachi's hand moves to his belt.

Malachi pulls his pistol and fires a shot into the air. The sharp bang of the gunshot echoes through the square, and silence falls over the crowd.

Lucius Creed rises from his chair and approaches the podium, a big smile spread across his face. "Dear citizens," he begins, nudging the police chief to the side, "our dear chief has called us to order. I hereby volunteer to take on Mr. Benedict's post until we can properly assess this situation. I'm sure it's just a misunderstanding. We, as the High Council, will always have your best interest in mind."

A wave of relief and adoration sweeps through the crowd. They erupt in applause, louder and more fervent than before. People cheer, some even calling out his name. Creed returns to his seat, smirking, basking in the worship.

The chief steps back to the podium. He grips the sides of the lectern, steadying himself. He clears his throat and brings the microphone closer. "Ladies and gentlemen, members of the High Council," he says, clearing his throat one more time, "today, in the Paracosm Ceremony, a testament to our city's strength and unity, I present to you, our prototypes."

Violet's gaze sweeps over the group of young men and women taking the stage. They stand next to the chief in a semi-circle, their postures ranging from rigidly disciplined to awkward and nervous.

Her eyes settle on the young man in the police academy uniform, standing at the center. His nose stands tall, radiating an air of superiority. His back is straight, the polished brass buttons of his uniform catching the light.

It's him.

Conrad.

"Stand by for Miss Lilith's speech," the chief instructs, nodding towards the minister, "while we prepare to escort our participants to their quarters. Please be grateful for their bravery and wish them a safe return from the Paracosm. Obey the Council."

"Survive the fog," the crowd replies in union.

Violet's eyes drift towards the clock tower, its looming presence always visible from any part of the city. She goes over her mental map of the crucial details from Dr. Parcel's file.

It's time.

She moves swiftly around the outside of the building, closing in on the exit. The van, parked in the rear lot, waits with the back doors open. Two guards, standing beside the vehicle, pretend to scan the surroundings as they chat with the driver. Violet takes a deep breath, her heart pounding, threatening to jump out of her chest.

As she approaches the guards, she adjusts her demeanor to a more casual posture. "Good morning," she says, forcing a big teethy smile. "I'm here to take your lunch orders."

The guards exchange puzzled glances. One of them, the shorter one with no hair, raises an eyebrow. "Isn't it a bit early for that?"

Violet hesitates for a split second, her mind racing. She takes a deep breath and presses on, drawing on the urgency of her mission. "The…The catering company," she stutters, "they don't want the soldiers to get scraps from the prototypes. You work so hard and deserve to eat first, gentlemen." The honorific forms a knot in her stomach, waves of nausea adding to her misery.

The guard's face softens, and a smirk plays on his lips. "Well, that's a first. We usually don't get this kind of attention."

"It's about time," the driver says. "We do work like dogs for the Council."

They begin to list their lunch orders—hearty sandwiches, fresh fruit, and bottles of water. Violet nods along, pretending to memorize them. The younger guard hands her a card. "Here's the access card. Just make sure you don't lose it. We're not supposed to let anyone in without proper authorization."

"Oh, don't worry. I'll lay low. I wouldn't want the inside guards to be jealous of your meals." She winks, taking the card with a smile. "I'll make sure everything is delivered hot and on time."

Their conversation drifts away as Violet approaches the door. She watches them for a moment before scanning her card on the electronic panel, releasing her breath when the scanner turns from blue to green.

Inside, the facility is a vast contrast to the chaos outside. Harsh fluorescent lights flicker overhead, casting a cold, clinical glow. The corridors are plain and practical, lined with metal doors and blank walls. The silence is punctuated only by the distant hum of machinery and the occasional clatter of footsteps.

Violet power walks, following the green line on the floor, her eyes scanning her surroundings for any sign of staff or security.

Blue for staff.

Red for the square.
White for armory.
Yellow for training camp.
Green for rooms.

As she approaches the door labeled as the prototype quarters, she pauses. The pass card feels heavy in her hand as she glances around, ensuring no one is watching.

She inserts the card into the reader, her fingers trembling. The card reader flashes, and Violet's heart sinks as the light shifts from blue to red. A jolt of panic surges through her. Her thoughts whirl in chaotic disarray—had she been caught? Was the card fake?

Her pulse thunders in her ears. Her palms grow slick with sweat, and she feels a cold rush of dread wash over her.

What do I do?

A faint, rhythmic click of high heels on the polished floor echoes through the corridors. Violet freezes, her entire body tensing as if bracing for a blow. She turns her head slowly, her gaze locking onto the approaching figure—a short woman in a white coat with red glasses perched on her nose.

Time seems to slow down as the woman gets closer. Violet's breath catches in her throat, her instincts screaming at her to run—but she remains static. Her mind races, trying to think of an excuse, a lie, anything.

The woman glances briefly at the door and then at Violet with a look of mild irritation. "Young lady," she says, clicking her tongue, "you're scanning your card upside down." Her voice is brisk but not unkind. "I swear this year's students can never remember the basics," she continues, her tone carrying an air of condescension as she continues walking. Her attention is clearly elsewhere.

Violet watches, still frozen, as the woman follows the blue line on the floor. Violet exhales deeply, legs shaking with residual tension. She reorients the card, and the door clicks open with a muted sound.

The corridor of the prototype quarters is a cold, sterile environment. The ceiling is covered in big round lights that cast an unusual white glow. The walls are a monotonous white, with nothing but a series of metal doors. Each door is marked with a small glass panel that holds a file on a slim, metal hook. There are no longer lines on the floor, only reflective gray tiles.

As Violet steps into the corridor, the shrill sound of a blaring alarm pierces through the silence. The lights flicker, shifting from their steady white to a pulsating red.

The intercom crackles to life, its voice deep and sharp.

"Attention: We have an intruder in the building. Do not panic. Do not take action. All prototypes are to remain in their rooms until further notice. The intruder is wearing peasant clothes and may try to pose as part of the catering company. If you have any information, please contact the security center immediately."

Panic takes over Violet as the announcement echoes through the corridor. Her pulse races, and she feels her breath coming in shallow, rapid bursts. Her mind races to find her target amidst the chaos. She sprints, her eyes darting across the doors, scanning the names on the files hanging beside each one.

The alarm's blare and the red lights are disorienting, causing the illusion that the hallway is warping into a pulsating and twisting room.

Found you.

Violet's hands shake as she fumbles with the card.

She inserts the card into the reader. The scanner blinks erratically, beeping as it changes to green. She holds her breath as she waits for the door to unlock.

With a click, the door opens. Violet slips inside, quickly closing it behind her. The sounds of the alarm and the intercom fade, muffled by the thick metal. The throbbing red lights from the corridor seep through the gap on the floor. She slides down, her back pressing against the door. She rests her head on her knees, struggling to steady her breathing.

Violet's breathing slows down, heart still pounding in her chest as she lifts her head to find Conrad in the room. He stands with an air of indifference, packing his backpack as if she didn't just barge in.

She rises to her feet. "Are you…" She stops, clearing her throat. "Are you Conrad Ashford?"

Conrad's gaze drifts to her for no more than a couple of seconds. "Yeah. And you're the intruder, I assume?"

Violet closes the distance between them, taking his backpack from his grip. "I'm here to get you out. Your parents—they want to save you."

"Save me?" He raises a single eyebrow. "They're just trying to control me. They think I'm too weak to handle things on my own."

So dramatic.

Violet rolls her eyes. "Look, whatever their reasons, we need to leave. Now. We're running out of time."

Conrad takes a few steps backwards, never breaking eye contact. "I'm sorry," he says, hand hovering over a red button on the phone panel mounted on the wall. "I'm not going anywhere," he adds, pressing the button.

The door behind her bursts open with a resounding crash. The sound of heavy boots pounding against the floor fills the room, accompanied by urgent shouts.

"This way!"

"Prototype number four!"

Violet's heart skips a beat. "What the *fuck* did you do?"

The room erupts into a blur of motions. Guards storm through the door, and she doesn't have time to register their movements before they're on her. Hands grasp her roughly, and she's tackled to the floor.

One guard grabs a handful of her hair, pulling her head back. Another guard takes out a hand scanner, positioning it over her face. The scanner emits a blinding warm blue light, and Violet squints against the intensity. The guard's other hand grips her wrist, holding it steady as the scanner sweeps across her features.

Violet squirms, trying to wiggle out of their grip, but they're bigger, stronger. Her vision narrows and the taste of warm copper fills her mouth as she gets hit on the back of her head. She bites her tongue, tasting her own blood. A sudden gush of pain jolts throughout her entire face.

Her vision blurs, her head spinning. The blue light flashes, then turns a sharp, glaring red. The guards talk among themselves, their voices sounding more and more distant.

"Boss, the scanner…"

"What's wrong with it?"

"It says she's been dead for five years."

Violet's body goes limp, and the world around her fades to black.

CHAPTER 4

VIOLET'S EYES FLUTTER open, black pressing in from all sides. She tries to blink, but the darkness remains, making her question whether her eyes are still closed. A distant, rhythmic pounding—her own heartbeat—echoes in her ears, slow and heavy.

She reaches her arms out, her movements sluggish, her limbs numb. Her hands brush against rough, splintered wood. Her fingers splay out, searching for space, but only meeting walls on all sides. The walls are close—too close.

A box?

A coffin?

The sound of her own breathing grows louder, more erratic, echoing off the confined space in a maddening loop. Her palms scrape and sting as she scrabbles against the splinters, her fingers clawing at the wooden planks that seem to close in tighter with every passing second.

A rhythmic pounding pulses through the walls once again. A sharp jab rattles the box, and Violet's head throbs with a sudden, piercing pain. The force of the impact sends a wave of dizziness over her, the world spinning in nauseating spirals.

It's from outside.

The thuds grow louder, more insistent, mingling with muffled voices. She slams her fists against the top piece. The wood is giving in, faint slivers of light seeping through the cracks.

The lid is wrenched open with a splintering crash. She shields her eyes with her arm, trying to adjust to the sudden brightness. Hands reach into the box, and Violet blinks faster, her eyes struggling to focus. She makes a feeble attempt to push them away but lacks the strength. The hands pull her from the box and she stumbles, her legs wobbly and weak.

As she stands, the world spins. Her surroundings are blurry. She looks around, and the police academy vanished. Instead, she sees a landscape of twisted trees and crumbling stone structures, bathed in a dim, gray light.

"Where am I?" The words escape her lips involuntarily.

"You're in the Paracosm." Violet's eyes come into focus to the girl standing in front of her. She's short and petite, her body almost devoured by the bright orange baggy sweatshirt she's wearing. She watches Violet with curious eyes and a big smile, her teeth looking extra white in contrast with her slick and long black hair. "I'm Yuka." She waves her hand so fast Violet worries she might actually throw up.

No…

As Yuka's words sink in, Violet's gaze drifts past her. The world comes into sharper focus. The hands holding her up loosen their grip, and as she trembles, she turns her head.

No…

It can't be.

To her right, the ruins spread out in a crumbling wasteland. Broken walls jut out at strange angles, and the remnants of buildings lie in a chaotic mess. Roofs are caved in, and the skeletal frames of what were once houses litter the ground. Dust hangs in the air, creating a yellow sandy fog of its own.

To her left, a forest so dense you can't see past the first line of trees. The ground is a jumbled mess of roots and dense undergrowth, with moss clinging to the gnarled trunks. The deeper she looks, the more the forest seems to close in.

The sky above, a disgusting shade of gray, uniform and unchanging. Its flat, lifeless color lacks any variation or depth.

Violet sinks to her knees. "I can't…" Her voice falters. "I can't stay here."

"Well, if you minded your own business, you wouldn't be here." Violet's gaze snaps up to meet Conrad's cold stare. A deep rage ignites in her chest. She lunges at him, only to be stopped by the same hands that held her up. Conrad smirks. "Oh, this rat has rabies," he says, a chuckle following his words.

Yuka walks up to her, pushing one of the guys holding her aside. "Don't worry, boys. I got her." She intertwines her arm with Violet's, looking up at her with large and shiny dark eyes. "What's your name?"

"I'm…" Violet tries to read Yuka's eyes. She looks for something, anything, but finds nothing. Yuka has the attitude and enthusiasm of a child, but wears a necklace of pink firecrackers around her neck with a strange, proud confidence. "I'm Violet."

"Hi, Violet. We thought you were a crate of food." Yuka giggles. "Anyway, don't listen to Conrad. He's so sour that half our friends already took off that way." Yuka gestures towards the forest with a casual sweep of her hand.

"They could have at least put some food in the box with her." Violet turns to see a burly man, wearing construction worker clothes and a yellow helmet under his arm, rummaging through the remnants of the crate.

Yuka laughs, the sound light and airy. "Don't be silly, Lorenzo. They wouldn't be that nice. Anyway, you're lucky we heard you breathing. You'd have suffocated in there." She giggles again. She pulls on Violet's arm and moves closer to Lorenzo.

Violet glances around. "How come there's no fog?" she asks, her voice still trembling

"The first wave won't come for a while," Lorenzo replies, his hands busy sifting through the slabs of wood from the crate. Dust clings to his clothes, and he brushes it off with a distracted sweep. "We were told we'd have twelve hours to prepare. The fog should roll in by sunset."

"And then what? We're supposed to just die in here?" Violet's eyes widen.

"You should meet the others!" Yuka lets go of her arm, sitting on the edge of the crate. "You see those two?" Yuka signs with a nod towards a pair of gingers, their pale skin stark against their vibrant hair. They are clearly twins, or at least siblings. Though it would be hard to decipher their age under so many layers of makeup and glitter, their bodies are in great shape. "Ellie and Elliot. We can't understand anything they say. They don't seem to understand us either."

"How come?" Violet asks. "We all speak the same language in St. Marrow."

"You're so silly. They're deaf. They do the little hand dances." Yuka slaps her knee while laughing, so hard she loses her balance and almost slips off the crate.

"It's called sign language, Yuka." A tall woman emerges from behind the crumbling remains of a wall. Her short, curly hair frames her face, her dark skin contrasting with the faded brown of her apron. She carries a small bundle of dried foliage, which she discards with a sigh. "I've been foraging, but I've never seen any of these plants before. All useless. How are you feeling, new girl?"

"I don't know… I don't really —"

"Her name's Violet," Yuka interrupts, her grin wide. "Like the flower."

"I'm Gemma." She wipes her hands on her apron before offering Violet a hand for a handshake. "I work with plants and herbs—or at least, I used to."

One of the men who had restrained Violet earlier steps forward, Conrad following right behind him. "We need a plan, everyone," he says.

Gemma shifts her weight from one foot to the other, her hands resting on her hips. "What do you suggest, Aiden?"

Aiden meets Violet's eyes briefly before turning his attention to the group. His gaze is steady, his demeanor calm but commanding. "We should start searching the structures of the abandoned houses. If any of them are intact, they could provide some good shelter."

Violet's frustration boils over. She thrusts a hand towards the ruins with a sweeping motion. "These houses? Are you insane? The fog will seep through the cracks."

Aiden's jaw tightens. "Oh, and what would you know about it?"

"More than a stuck-up city boy, for sure."

Aiden's eyes narrow as he takes a deep breath. "If you want to wander into the forest and get yourself killed, be my guest."

Yuka, still sitting on the edge of a crate, swings her legs back and forth. "Don't be such a meanie, Aiden. The forest is way more fun."

"Plus, we could find useful plants for medicine and food. The ruins don't offer any resources. Trust me, I've been looking since we got here," Gemma says, adjusting the strap of her apron.

Aiden's gaze shifts from Violet to Gemma. "You have no shelter. The monsters will get to you in seconds."

"We can build a shelter. I'll help." Lorenzo offers, easily breaking a wood plank in half with his hands.

Aiden takes half of the plank from Lorenzo's hand and throws it away. The rotten piece of wood disintegrates as it hits a decaying pillar. "I've been doing survival training my whole life. I know what I'm talking about."

Violet closes the distance between herself and Aiden, their faces inches apart. Her eyes lock onto his, defiant. "And I've been fighting for survival every day of my life."

Aiden's gaze remains steady, unflinching. His jaw tightens, and his breathing grows shallow. Violet's chest rises and falls rapidly, her breaths coming in short, sharp bursts. Aiden's fists tighten at his sides, his knuckles whitening.

"Ignore her, Aiden." Conrad's voice cuts through the silence, rolling his eyes. "She's just a rat."

Aiden's eyes flicker towards Conrad, then back to Violet. A smirk plays at the corners of his mouth. "Looks more like a little mouse to me."

With a swift motion, Aiden turns his back on the group and heads toward the ruins, Conrad trailing behind him. The two of them move away, their footsteps crunching on the debris.

Idiots.

Violet's gaze sweeps over the group. "Has anyone checked out the forest?" she asks.

Lorenzo scratches his head under his helmet. "Most of the prototypes left on their own as soon as the van dropped us off. A few of them towards the woods."

"Two of them mentioned finding some log cabins deeper in the forest. They left a trail," Gemma says as she points towards the tangled trees, the path barely visible amidst the dense foliage.

Violet nods. "Thank you." Without another word, she strides to the forest, powder from the dry earth forming little clouds around her boots.

Yuka runs up beside her, her eyes gleaming and blinking rapidly. "This is gonna be so much fun!" she chirps, her firecracker necklace flickering through the dim light as she dances around.

"What are you doing?" Violet asks.

"What? We're coming with you, silly!" Yuka's grin is infectious, so much that the corner of Violet's lips threatens to turn into a smile of her own.

Lorenzo slings a few wood planks over his shoulder and follows. "It's rare that people survive the Paracosm. But the ones who did weren't alone."

Gemma falls into step behind them, her eyes scanning the overgrown trail. "This way," she directs, her voice firm but kind. She leads the group towards the forest's edge, pushing aside scrubs and low-hanging branches.

As they cross into the forest, the world transforms. The green coating overhead thickens, blocking out the monotonous gray sky. Shafts of pale light filter through the leaves, casting an eerie glow on the grass. The air grows cooler, heavy with the earthy aroma of damp soil and rotting leaves.

Trees rise like watchtowers, their crooked trunks enveloped in a cloak of moss. Vines drape down like curtains, weaving between the trees and forming a messy web of green. The ground beneath them is uneven, covered in a tangle of roots and fallen branches.

"Watch your step, everyone," Gemma says.

The rustling of leaves and the occasional snap of a twig punctuate the silence, creating a symphony of nature's whispers.

"I hope there are no bugs," Lorenzo says, scratching his neck with his free hand. "I hate bugs."

Violet's eyes remain sharp, scanning their surroundings. Her senses are heightened, absorbing the dense, suffocating atmosphere of the forest. Every rustle, every shadow seems alive.

I'm not gonna die in here.

Gemma leads them further into the forest as she follows the faint path left by the other prototypes. The trail meanders through the trees, sometimes barely noticeable, hidden beneath a layer of fallen leaves.

"Aw, much better." Yuka flickers a little lighter between her small fingers. "I can't wait to see some orange ladybugs. They're my favorite."

"Stop that." Gemma takes the lighter away, hiding it inside her front pocket. "You're gonna start a fire with this thing."

"But it's so dark, Gemma," Yuka whines.

The deeper they venture, the more the forest seems to close in around them. The trees lean in, their branches intertwining overhead to form a living canopy. The air grows thick, and the light sparser.

"It's here," Violet says, seeing the cabin as she moves a branch out of the way.

The cabin stands half-hidden among the trees, its wooden walls weathered and gray. The structure is small, its single story leaning slightly to one side. The roof is slanted, and the chimney, topped with a tangle of ivy, is silent and still.

The front door is framed by a sagging porch, its wooden planks uneven and worn, creaking softly under their weight. The door itself is solid and thick, not a single crack in sight.

Yuka bounces up the few steps to the porch and grasps the door handle. She tugs and twists, her face scrunching with effort, but the door does not budge. "Come on, open up!" she urges, sticking her tongue out.

Lorenzo glances at his watch, pressing a small button on its side to light up the screen. "We have about five hours until the fog rolls in," he says, his brow furrowing.

Shit.

We need to hurry.

Violet gently moves Yuka to the side. She places her hand on the handle. She puts her shoulder into it, bracing her weight against the door, but it remains stubbornly shut.

Come on.

Open.

She tries again, pushing and pulling with all her strength. The wood of the door creaks softly, as if mocking her. Violet steps back, her breath coming in brief, loud spurts.

"It won't open," she says.

CHAPTER 5

LORENZO SETS HIS wood planks down with a quiet thud. "Let me give it a try," he says. He motions for Violet and the others to step back, his broad shoulders tensing as he squares up to the door.

He runs at the door, his boots pounding against the porch, causing it to vibrate. As he collides with the door, the entire cabin shudders under the impact, its wooden frame creaking in protest. The walls tremble, sending a cascade of dust and splinters falling from the eaves. The air fills with the pungent scent of old wood, mingled with the mustiness of rot, as if the cabin itself were exhaling a long-held breath.

Lorenzo throws his weight against the door again, his shoulder smashing into it with a resounding blow. The door creaks and moans, but it doesn't budge. Lorenzo grunts, his face flushed, and he tries again, this time kicking at the base with his heel—but still nothing.

"Now what?" Yuka paces restlessly. "I'm bored," she says as she stomps her foot and peers at the others with a frown.

"There should be other cabins," Gemma responds, her gaze shifting between the forest and the door. "But this is the only one with a trail."

Lorenzo, breathing heavily, straightens up and wipes the sweat from his forehead with the back of this hand. "We could break one of the walls and make our own door," he says.

As Lorenzo examines the walls, a gasp pierces the air.

Lorenzo steps back, his expression a mix of concern and confusion. "Did anyone else hear that?" he asks, his voice barely above a whisper.

"Please don't!" The scream echoes from inside the cabin. Lorenzo, Gemma, and Yuka freeze, their eyes wide. Violet's heart skips a beat, her breath catching in her throat as she looks at the door.

The sound of shifting furniture pierces the tense silence. The heavy scrape of wood against wood follows, mixed with the metallic clink of locks turning. The door suddenly swings open, revealing a short, skinny boy standing in the threshold.

"Liam?" Gemma and Lorenzo exclaim in unison.

"Liam!" Yuka's voice is a burst of excitement, her face lighting up with a wide grin.

Liam's eyes dart around, looking past them into the depths of the forest. "Hurry, get inside!" he urges, stepping aside to let them in.

As the group rushes inside, Liam slams the door shut behind them. He scrambles to drag two tables from the interior, struggling to stack them one on top of the other to barricade the door. The wood groans under the pressure, and the sound of furniture scraping against the floor fills the small space, blending with Liam's strenuous breaths.

"You couldn't hear us from the outside?" Violet asks, raising a single eyebrow.

Liam's hands tremble as he adjusts the makeshift barricade. "I… I could," he stammers, his voice cracking. "But I didn't know if the monsters could imitate voices. I was so scared and didn't know what to do and—"

"Fine." Violet cuts him off. "It's fine." She glances around the dimly lit interior of the cabin. The walls are lined with dusty wooden panels, and the air inside is stale, carrying a faint, musty odor.

Liam finishes his barrier, the tables now firmly blocking the door and all the locks turned. He slumps against them, breathing heavily, his gaze shifting between the group and the door as if expecting it to burst open at any moment.

Gemma looks around the small cabin, her eyes landing on Liam with concern. "Where are the others?" she asks.

Liam's shoulders slump as he shakes his head. "We all got separated while searching the forest. We were supposed to meet up back at the ruins, but everything looks the same out there. When I couldn't find them, I just followed the trail here."

Violet's gaze sweeps over the room, taking in the gaps where the wooden walls and floorboards don't quite meet. "We need to cover the gaps," she says.

"What gaps?" Lorenzo's brow furrows as he inspects the cabin's structure. "The cabin is built solid."

"The fog," Violet replies. "It works similar to the wind from my village. It will seep through even the smallest gap." Violet pinches her thumb and index finger together with little to no space between them.

"What do we do?" Liam's eyes dart around, as if suddenly aware of all the gaps and cracks of the wood. "What can we do?"

"We need to insulate this place," Violet insists, her voice firm. "With anything we can find—clothing, blankets, or even more wood. We have to make sure the fog can't get in."

Gemma nods in agreement. "I've got some old rags and a few pieces of cloth. We can use those."

Lorenzo starts rummaging through the cabin's sparse furnishings, pulling out anything that might be useful. Yuka grabs pieces of tissue and tries to wedge them into the gaps.

Violet joins in, her movements precise. She stuffs and secures the materials into the cracks as the others keep searching for more. Her hands work methodically. It's no different than back at the village—patching up homes after storms, mending the damage with whatever materials at hand.

The interior of the cabin converts into a cocoon of makeshift protection. The sounds from outside—the distant rustling of the forest, the occasional whisper of wind—grow fainter, diminishing with each layer they add.

This should do it.

"How long until the fog, Lorenzo?" Violet asks.

Lorenzo gazes at his watch. "About an hour."

The group gathers in the center of the cabin, settling into a cluster of mismatched chairs, a faded rug, and a sagging, worn-out couch. Gemma takes off her apron, the fabric rustling as she rummages through its many pockets. She takes out a small key.

With a quick twist, Gemma uses it to open the safety lock of her backpack. She reaches inside, retrieving a handful of meal bars.

"Here," Gemma says, handing a bar to Violet. "I have enough for everyone."

Yuka's eyes light up with a childlike delight as she accepts her bar, tearing it open with eagerness. She takes a bite, the bar crumbling and scattering crumbs across her face. "You really keep all kinds of things in there, Gemma!" she says, giggling between mouthfuls.

Violet watches her, a small smile tugging at the corner of her lips. She twirls her own meal bar between her fingers, the wrapper crinkling softly.

Her mind drifts to Ingrid's warm smile, the way her eyes crinkle at the corners when she laughs. She can almost hear her voice, soothing and steady, calling out to her. Right now, she's probably bustling around the kitchen, her shaky hands struggling to prepare a meal while the children gather around her. She wonders if Ethan has managed to keep the household together, and if Rosie's fever has finally broken.

"Violet," Lorenzo's voice cuts through her thoughts, pulling her back to reality. "What about you? Why are you here?"

"I don't remember seeing you during training camp," Liam adds.

Violet takes a deep breath, the taste of regret coating her tongue. "I'm here because of Dr. Parcel," she says. "I was hired to rescue Conrad."

Gemma chokes on her food. "Dr. Parcel? As in High Council Dr. Parcel?" Her eyes widen as she flaps her own chest for relief.

"Yes," Violet confirms, nodding. "I was sent to find Conrad and bring him back. His parents hired Dr. Parcel's services, and Dr. Parcel hired me."

Liam runs a hand through his hair, his gaze shifting from Violet to the rest of the group. "That's… significant. I didn't realize he hired… You know…"

"Rats?" Violet shrugs as Liam's cheeks turn a darker shade of pink. "Well, this is not exactly how I imagined my day going, but here we are."

They chew silently for what feels like eternity, the air growing heavy with awkwardness and tension. Gemma's fingers drum impatiently on her thigh, while Yuka's playful grin returns as she keeps devouring her bar.

Eventually, conversation flows between them, the mundane chatter offering a brief break from their fears. Yuka recounts stories from her days as a street performer, her animated gestures filling the room with an oddly comforting chaos. Gemma, with a nostalgic smile, shares memories from her time in the High Council laboratories—tales of exotic flowers, intricate seed experiments, and the delicate art of nurturing rare plants. Her eyes light up as she describes the vibrant colors and unique scents. Liam and Lorenzo listen with half-hearted attention, occasionally interjecting with stories of their own.

Violet remains quiet and distant, her thoughts a whirlwind of uneasiness. The walls of the cabin seem to close in, their creaks and groans louder with every passing second. Her gaze drifts around the room, settling on the dark corners. The meal bar in her hand remains untouched, becoming a mere distraction as her mind wanders back to her haunting day.

Lorenzo's watch emits a soft beep, slicing through the conversation like a blade. "It's time," he says.

"I don't hear anything," Yuka says as she stands, her eyes wide with curiosity as she moves towards the door.

Before Yuka can move a single step, Gemma's hand shoots out, pulling her back. "Stay down," Gemma says, guiding Yuka back to the dusty rug on the floor.

Violet's eyes dart to the door. Her thoughts circle back to the chilling quiet, punctuated only by the echoing screams of her parents. Silence had enveloped her world then, just as it does now.

"It's silent," Violet says, her voice barely above a whisper, a shiver running down her spine.

Liam's expression turns somber as he exchanges a worried glance with Lorenzo. Yuka's enthusiasm falters, her playful demeanor melting away. The room grows still, the only sound the soft rustling of the wrappers as they are set aside.

The cabin's interior grows dimmer as the fuel of the oil lamp runs low. Yuka yawns, her eyes drooping as exhaustion catches up with her. She stretches her arms, letting out a small, tired giggle. "I'm so tired," she admits, slurring her words.

"I could use some sleep too," Liam says.

Lorenzo shakes his head. "I don't think I'll be able to sleep."

"In my village, there are always a few people on guard shifts," Violet says, turning the pile of pillows and blankets into a makeshift bed. "It's a precaution, since we're so close to the fog."

Liam looks up, his face pale. "It's one thing to be close to the fog," he says quietly, his voice shaking, "and another thing to be right in the middle of it."

"None of us have seen the monsters before," she counters, her voice firm. "We don't know what they're capable of, or if this cabin is even safe."

Lorenzo nods, heavy breathing while moving the furniture away from the door. "She has a point," he says. He shifts his weight, the wood beneath him creaking softly under his boots. "I'll do it."

Yuka, with her eyes barely open, raises her hand with a wide grin. "I'll do it! I can keep guard outside!"

Gemma points her index finger towards the couch. "You can sleep here."

Violet's eyes flicker between Yuka and Liam as Yuka jumps on the couch, falling face first onto one of the pillows. "Liam should do it," she says. "You explored the forest before we got into the cabin. You're more familiar with where to look."

Liam's face pales further, eyes widening. "No way," he stammers. "What if something happens out there? None of us should go."

"You can just come inside if you see something."

Liam's eyes shift to the door and then back to the group, swallowing his own saliva with an audible gulp.

"It's ok, I'll do it. I got these bodyguards with me at all times," Lorenzo says, kissing his right bicep while flexing both arms.

The cabin settles into the silence of the approaching night. The fuel of the oil lamp has been refilled, but the light manually dimmed.

Gemma kneels on the floor, her massive backpack open in front of her like a treasure chest. The bag, worn from use, bulges with numerous pockets and compartments. As she begins to unpack, her movements are precise and methodical, almost ritualistic. She pulls out a thick plant book first, its cover faded and corners dog-eared, and sets it down gently. Next, she retrieves several small vials filled with clear liquids, arranging them in a neat line beside the book.

The soft rustle of fabric and the occasional clink of metal blend with Liam's soft snores and the muffled sound of wind from the outside. She reaches into a compartment at the bottom of the bag, her hand disappearing for a moment before pulling out a small, tightly sealed container. She pauses for a fraction of a second, her eyes flicking over the items spread out before her.

"How do you carry such a big backpack around all the time?" Violet asks, her voice low, careful not to disturb the others.

Gemma glances up, a small smile tugging at the corners of her lips. "I'm used to it," she replies. "This is nothing compared to what I used to bring to work every day." She laughs softly.

Violet studies her for a moment, noting how Gemma's hands, usually steady and precise, linger for just a beat too long over the items she's placed on the floor. "Do you need help packing everything back up?" she offers.

Gemma's smile falters, her gaze snapping up to meet Violet's. For a brief second, something sharp flickers in her eyes, but it vanishes as quickly as it appeared. "No," she says, a little too quickly, her tone tightening. "I've got it. I prefer to do it myself—it's… a system, you know? Everything has its place."

She resumes packing, her movements now a touch more hurried. The vials are slipped back into their padded compartment, the plant book tucked away without much care.

Lorenzo clears his throat. "Look, I'm obviously not going to be able to keep guard all night," he says, his deep voice cutting through the quiet. "We need someone to exchange shifts with me."

"I can—" Violet starts.

Yuka, who had been lounging on the couch, perks up immediately. "I'll do it!" she interrupts, her hand shooting up enthusiastically, as if she's volunteering for a game.

Violet's eyes shift between Yuka and the heavy, solid wood door. "Yuka, I'm not sure you'd be able to get inside fast enough," she says.

"I can! I promise I can!" Yuka nods eagerly, a wide grin spreading across her face. "I'm the best hide and seek player in the whole world!" she boasts, her voice bubbling with excitement. "Nothing can catch me!"

Gemma frowns. "I don't know about this," she says.

Lorenzo shifts his stance, crossing his arms over his chest as he considers Yuka's eager expression. "If I think it's not safe, I won't let her out," he says firmly, his gaze meeting Gemma's.

Gemma hesitates, her lips pressed into a thin line as she weighs the situation. "Alright," she exhales, though her expression suggests she's still not entirely convinced. "But be careful. Both of you."

Yuka's grin widens, and she gives Lorenzo a playful salute. "You got it, boss!"

Yuka, her earlier excitement now translating into frenetic energy, zips around the cabin. She bumps into chairs and stumbles over the edges of blankets, her laughter bubbling up in a high-pitched, gleeful sound that fills the room. But as suddenly as it began, Yuka's energy wanes. She collapses onto the couch with a soft thud, her eyes fluttering closed. In moments, she is out cold, her body curled up like a cat in the middle of a deep, peaceful sleep.

Lorenzo stands by the door, adjusting the strap of his lantern over his shoulder and slipping a couple of extra batteries into his pocket. "Well, wish me luck," he says with a half-smile, glancing at Gemma and Violet.

"Good luck," Gemma replies. She gives him a small nod, her eyes lingering on his.

"Be careful out there," Violet adds. Her gaze follows Lorenzo as he tightens his grip around the lantern, testing the light with a few clicks.

"I'll be fine," Lorenzo says with a grin, though it falters as he turns towards the door. He reaches for the handle, pausing just long enough to give them one last reassuring look. "I'll be back before you know it."

As he opens the door, a rush of cool, damp air sweeps into the cabin, carrying with it the heavy scent of earth and something faintly metallic. The fog, thick and swirling, lies just beyond the threshold.

Violet catches a brief glimpse of the fog as the door opens wider. It's denser than the one beyond the village limits, a mass of pale, shifting waves that seem to pulse and squirm in the darkness. The fog appears almost alive, its ghostly fingers reaching out, curling around the trees and brushing against the ground as if searching for something—or someone. The air itself feels thick, as though the fog is weighing it down, making it harder to breathe.

Lorenzo steps out into the night, the lantern casting a small, warm glow around him. He leaves the door slightly ajar behind him for a few seconds, the faint creak of the hinges echoing in the quiet. The click of the latch settling into place is the last sound before the silence returns, almost as heavy as the fog itself.

Violet remains fixed on the door, uneasiness creeping up her spine. The image of the fog lingers in her mind. The cabin feels even smaller now, as if the fog is pressing in on all sides.

"Keep it unlocked," Lorenzo's voice comes through, muffled but firm from the other side of the door. "Just in case."

"Got it," Violet replies, her voice barely above a whisper.

Violet exchanges glances with Gemma. She gives one final nod as she settles onto her makeshift bed, her body sinking into the thin, lumpy mattress. The padding offers little support, but it's a welcome change from the hard floor. She tugs at the edges of her blanket, smoothing out the creases in a futile attempt to find some comfort. The fabric is rough against her skin, but she wraps it tightly around her, seeking any semblance of warmth.

As she lays down, the darkness of the cabin seems to grow deeper, the shadows thickening around her. Her mind begins to race, every sound amplified in the stillness of the night. The cabin groans as it settles, the wooden beams creaking as if shifting under the weight of the fog. Outside, the rustling of leaves stirs, the sound mingling with the occasional distant snap of a twig.

Violet stretches her legs out, her feet slipping out from under the blanket. A shiver runs through her, the cold air biting at her exposed skin. Her thoughts begin to spiral, delving into the dark rumors she's heard about the monsters.

They say the monsters have hollow eyes, empty voids that reflect no light, no life—just endless darkness. Their skin is pale and stretched taut over their bones, almost translucent, with veins pulsing just beneath the surface. Some claim their limbs are unnaturally long, with fingers that taper into sharp, claw-like nails capable of ripping through flesh with a single swipe. Others whisper of mouths filled with rows of jagged teeth, capable of tearing through bone and muscle with terrifying ease. The most chilling rumor, though, is that the monsters can mimic voices, luring their prey into the fog with the familiar calls of loved ones.

Violet's heart pounds in her chest, the images vivid in her mind. She squeezes her eyes shut, trying to push the thoughts away, but the monsters loom larger, their presence almost tangible in the dark corners of the cabin. Her breathing quickens, each inhale sharp and shallow as she fights to keep her fear at bay.

She forces herself to focus on the rhythmic breathing of her companions, the steady rise and fall of their chests being somewhat comforting.

As the minutes tick by, Violet's exhaustion begins to creep in, overriding her fear. Her limbs grow heavy, her thoughts slowing as the weight of sleep tugs at her consciousness. The sounds of the night fade into the background, her focus narrowing to the soothing pace of her own breath.

With a final, deep exhale, Violet's tense muscles relax, her body finally surrendering to the pull of sleep.

CHAPTER 6

VIOLET STIRS, EYES fluttering open to a room still dark and silent. The soft rise and fall of her companions' breathing is the only movement visible in the dim light.

Yuka?

Yuka's small frame is still curled up on the couch, blankets tangled around her legs. Panic shoots through Violet like ice water. She pushes herself up from her makeshift bed, heart pounding in her chest.

"Yuka," she hisses, shaking her shoulder with increasing urgency. "Yuka, wake up!"

Yuka stirs, eyes half-open. "Huh?" she mumbles.

"Why aren't you on guard?" Violet's voice wavers, her mind racing with worst-case scenarios. "Where's Lorenzo?" She grips Yuka's arm a little tighter.

Yuka rubs her eyes, remnants of sleep still thick in her voice. "Didn't see Lorenzo... so tired... went back to sleep," she mumbles, her head flopping back onto the couch cushion.

Violet loosens her grip. "What?" she whispers.

Violet grabs one of Lorenzo's flashlights, strapping it around her waist. Her fingers tremble as she reaches for the doorknob. She twists it all the way, cracking the door open. Her breath gets caught in her throat, bracing for the thick, suffocating fog.

She pushes the door wider, and the fog is nowhere to be seen. The air outside is clear, the heavy mist that trapped them inside all night now gone. Light filters through the trees, but the sky above remains a dull, lifeless gray. It's brighter, yes, but the same endless gray stretches as far as she can see, offering no hint of time or safety.

Violet steps out, scanning the quiet. The clearing where the cabin sits is empty, still, and no different than yesterday.

Where is Lorenzo?

Her eyes dart around, searching for any sign of Lorenzo. She steps out further, scanning the tree line, the empty stretch of ground around the cabin, but there's no trace of him.

"Lorenzo?" she calls softly at first, her voice barely above a whisper.

The name hangs in the air, swallowed by silence. She takes another step, her boots crunching against damp leaves.

"Lorenzo!" she calls again, louder this time.

No response. The trees stand tall and silent, their branches motionless, as if holding their breath. The gray sky above seems to press down on her, indifferent, offering no answers.

Did he fall asleep somewhere?

Violet rounds the corner of the cabin, her eyes sweeping over the ground, half-expecting to see him leaning against the wall or emerging from the woods—but all she finds is more emptiness.

"Lorenzo!" she shouts, her voice now quivering from desperation. She circles the entire cabin, her steps quickening as panic starts to take hold.

She completes the circle, ending up back where she started. The clearing remains empty—and Lorenzo is gone.

Maybe he went back to the ruins.

Violet steps onto the trail, the one that snakes back into the ruins. She rounds the first bend, not that far away from the cabin, and she spots a body sprawled face down on a large rock up ahead.

Lorenzo.

He's lying face down, motionless. At first, it seems as if he might have tripped and fallen, hitting his head on the rock. But something feels—and smells—off. Violet approaches, her steps slow and hesitant, a knot tightening in her stomach.

She kneels beside him, her hands trembling as she tries to turn his body over. His weight offers some resistance, and as she struggles, she notices it—the blood. A lot of it. It stains the rock beneath him, seeping into the cracks, pooling in the dirt around them.

With a grunt, she manages to shift him. As his body rolls over, his face peels away from the rock with a sticky sound. The slimy old blood holds it in place, leaving remnants of skin and flesh behind.

Lorenzo's face is a grotesque sight. The surface is mangled, torn apart, and smashed beyond recognition. It's as if someone—or something—had repeatedly bashed his head into the rock over and over again. His features are barely distinguishable, reduced to a horrific mess of blood, bone, and muscle. One of his eyes is gone, lost in the mush, and his jaw hangs at an unnatural angle.

Violet recoils, her breath catching in her throat as a wave of nausea washes over her. She stumbles back, her mind struggling to process the brutality of it all.

Lorenzo is dead.

She staggers backwards, bitterness rising in her throat. The image of his mutilated face is seared into her mind. She doubles over, falling to her knees, and vomits onto the ground, her body convulsing.

The world around her blurs, colors and shapes blending together as if the forest is spinning. Her ears ring, muffling every sound—nothing feels real.

Guilt crashes over her like a wave. It was her idea. She was the one who insisted on keeping a guard, the one who suggested they take turns. She thought it would keep them safe, thought it was the right thing to do. Now Lorenzo is dead, and it's her fault.

Violet stares at the ground, unable to look at his body again. The weight of her words crushes her, leaving her breathless and overwhelmed.

I did this.

I killed him.

"Violet!"

Gemma's voice calls out from the distance, breaking through the haze of her mind. The sound is faint, but it's enough to pull her back to her senses. Panic tightens her chest. Gemma is coming. She's going to see this—see Lorenzo's body, the blood, the horror of it all.

"Lorenzo!" Gemma calls out, her voice still distant.

I killed him.

Guilt swallows her whole. What will they think? Will they blame her? Her mind races, searching for a way to explain, to make them understand. But no words come. Only the cold, sinking realization that she's responsible for this. She killed him.

I killed him.

I killed him.

I killed him.

Violet sprints deeper into the forest, her feet pounding against the uneven ground. She doesn't know where she's going—only that she needs to get away, as far as possible, as fast as possible. The trees blur into a monotonous wall of gray and brown, each one identical to the last. The forest seems endless, a maze where every direction feels the same, where every step might be leading her in circles.

She doesn't stop, doesn't even slow down, until her foot catches on a gnarled root that juts and twists out from a pile of dry leaves. She stumbles, arms flailing, and crashes to the ground with a heavy thud.

A sob tears from her throat, raw and uncontrollable. She curls up, her body shaking with the force of her cries. She coughs, her throat burning as mucus bubbles up, choking her. The tears won't stop. They blur her vision, mixing with the dirt on her face.

After what feels like an eternity, the sobs begin to subside, leaving her drained and hollow. Slowly, she forces herself to her feet, her legs unsteady. She wipes at her face with dirty hands, smearing the mud and tears across her skin. Brushing off the leaves and dust clinging to her clothes, she stands there, lost and broken, the forest around her silent and indifferent.

Violet's frustration boils over as she glares at the monotonous forest. Her fists clench by her sides, and she kicks the root that tripped her in a burst of anger. As her foot connects, the ground beneath her shifts. The root snaps back, and a hidden net unfolds from the dirt, entangling her legs and pulling tight.

She gasps as the net tightens around her, hoisting her off the ground. The coarse fibers dig into her skin, and she dangles from the tree, her feet barely brushing the forest floor. Her heart races, and she struggles against the bonds of the net, trying to free herself.

The net wriggles and shifts with every movement she makes, the more she squirms, the tighter it seems to become. She tries to reach for the knife strapped to her leg, but the handle is just out of her grasp.

Her movements are jerky and frantic, sweat beads forming on her forehead as she struggles. The tree branches above sway slightly with the tension of the net, casting erratic shadows over her face.

"Oh. It's you." Aiden appears from the dense foliage, his silhouette sharp against the muted green of the forest. He raises an eyebrow, his voice laced with delight. "Thought I heard some noise."

Violet rolls her eyes and continues to struggle against the net. Her hands are slick with sweat, and the rope texture from the net seems to burn her skin with every movement.

Aiden steps closer, looking up at her. "Need some help?" He flicks the hanging rope that secures the net, a smirk painted onto his face. "It's not my first time freeing a little mouse from a trap."

Violet glares at the ground. "No. I can do it myself," she says through her teeth.

"Alright. Be stubborn." Aiden's voice is a mix of disbelief and amusement as he disappears behind the tree.

The tree branch creaks and cracks, the net shifting beneath Violet's weight. Her heart races as the tension in the ropes give way. With a sudden snap, the net breaks loose, sending her plummeting towards the earth.

She squeezes her eyes shut, bracing for the impact—but it never comes. Instead, she feels a firm grip encircling her, keeping her from hitting the ground.

Violet's eyes snap open, and she's met with Aiden's face, far too close for comfort. His usual smirk is plastered on his lips, his grip steady and annoyingly confident. "I figured there was a trick to it," he says. "The twins always had a flair for traps."

Violet freezes for a second, suspended in his arms. She can feel the warmth of his breath against her cheek, the strength of his arms around her.

She wriggles free from his grip and stumbles as she stands. Her cheeks are flushed, though she's not sure if it's from the near fall or the humiliating realization that Aiden had just saved her.

Violet straightens her back and clears her throat. "I didn't need your help, you know," she mutters, trying to regain her composure, even as she avoids meeting his eyes.

Aiden crosses his arms over his chest. "That's not what it looked like. You seemed pretty tangled up."

Violet narrows her eyes at him. "Well, maybe I didn't *want* your help."

"Suit yourself." Aiden's gaze lingers on her for a moment, a smirk playing on his lips. "Do you want me to put you back up?"

She shoots him a glare, annoyance bubbling beneath her skin. "Just…Get out of my sight. I'm not in the mood."

Aiden chuckles, shaking his head. "Alright, little mouse. Just don't go getting yourself killed out here. I'd hate to have to come rescue you again." He turns on his heel, creating a rustle of crunching leaves that grows fainter as he walks away.

Killed.

Dead.

Lorenzo.

Violet swallows hard, fighting back the bile rising in her throat. She gags, the urge to vomit almost overwhelming her. With a shaky breath, she manages to force it down, her chest heaving as she struggles to keep her composure.

There has to be a way out of this place.

Out of the Paracosm.

Violet crouches, her movements stiff from the panic. She reaches down, carefully retrieving her knife from the trap's tangled net. The blade is scratched but still sharp. She uses it to cut away the remaining snags of the net around her feet.

With the knife safely returned to its sheath, she straightens up, her thoughts racing.

I can't keep walking around in circles.

I don't know when the fog is coming back.

She scans the trees around her, their monotonous, gray and green bark blending into the endless forest. The sight is disorienting, confusing.

Violet tests the blade of her knife against the rough bark of a nearby tree, pressing in firmly to see if it will leave a visible mark. The steel bites into the wood, carving a shallow line that stands out against the dark bark. Satisfied that the blade is strong enough and the markings will be visible on the trees, she begins numbering them.

She works methodically, numbering each tree in sequence. The marks are subtle and hard to see from a distance, but enough for her to distinguish one from another.

As she moves forward, she keeps a close eye on her surroundings. Whenever she encounters a marked tree, she changes direction, ensuring she's not retracing her steps. Her heart races with each turn, the repetitive pattern of the trees threatening and overwhelming.

Violet pushes through the dense foliage, her clothes snagging on low-hanging branches. The underbrush scratches at her skin, and she winces with each step. The tangled greenery thins out, revealing a familiar clearing ahead. She pauses, her breath catching as she recognizes the stone ruins. The crumbling structures stand silent and still, just as they did yesterday.

Violet steps cautiously around the perimeter of the ruins, her eyes searching for anything that might offer shelter. The stone walls, worn and cracked, are partially covered in vines, their green tendrils weaving through the crevices. Moss coats the ground, softening her footsteps and giving the place a forgotten, almost hidden quality.

She carefully picks her way through the rubble, pushing aside loose doors and shifting through scattered debris. A thick layer of dust and grime covers everything, and the air carries a faint, musty odor that mingles with the scent of decaying leaves. As she moves deeper, the remains of what was once alive become more evident—broken pieces of pottery, shards of glass, and fragments of rusted metal litter the ground.

Violet scans the area, her mind focused on finding some sort of shelter. As she absently kicks at the ground, her foot nudges a cluster of stones. At first, they seem ordinary, blending into the landscape. But one stone stands out—a bit larger, more angular, and oddly out of place compared to the others.

Curious, she kneels and runs her fingers over its surface. It appears to be like any other stone, but something feels off. With a bit of effort, she rocks it gently. To her surprise, it shifts easier than expected. She knocks on it, and the sound vibrates and echoes, as if the insides of the rock are hollowed out.

She grabs a sturdy slab of wood and uses it as a lever, prying the stone away from its resting place. It comes free with a muffled groan, revealing a dark opening beneath. The entrance is a bit of a tight squeeze, but she manages to wedge her way into the hollow space. The passage below is narrow and steep, leading down into the ground.

The tunnel is old and musty, the air thick with the scent of damp dirt. Her flashlight flickers, casting jagged, shifting shadows along the rough stone walls. The stones feel cold and slick beneath her fingers as she holds on to the wall for balance.

She can taste the earth in the back of her throat. The damp air clings to her skin, leaving a cold, clammy residue that makes her shiver. As she edges forward, the ground shifts beneath her feet, each step sending a gritty cascade of loose gravel crunching under her boots. The sound reverberates into the pitch-black void ahead, the echoes fading into the depths of the tunnel.

As she ventures deeper, the tunnel branches off into several directions. Some passages are blocked with debris, but others appear to have been maintained.

She hesitates at one of the clearer passages, the beam of her flashlight cutting through the gloom to reveal walls that are less rough, the stone more evenly cut, as if someone had taken care to keep this section in order.

Her light catches on something further ahead—an indentation in the wall, like a small nook. Nestled within are folded blankets, their edges worn, stacked alongside a few rusted cans of food and plastic bottles of water, their labels peeling with age.

Does someone live here?

Violet kneels down, running her fingers over the supplies. The blankets are thin, but they feel dry and dusty. The cans are heavy in her hands, the labels barely legible, but the thought of food—any food—is enough to make her mouth water despite her unease. The water bottles, too, feel like a lifeline, though she can't help but wonder how long they've been sitting there, and whether they're still safe to drink.

No.

No one has been here in a long time.

Still, someone had been here, and the supplies are possibly older than she'd like to think, hiding away in this forgotten place. The thought is both comforting and unsettling. Comforting, because it means she might have found a refuge, a place to hide when the fog rolls back in. Unsettling, because it raises questions—who had been here, and why did they leave these supplies behind?

She spots an old backpack among the stash of supplies and quickly pulls it out. The backpack is worn and dusty, but it seems sturdy enough to hold what she needs. She sets it on the ground, and as she empties it, the backpack falls open with a soft thud.

The contents of the bag scatter around her—a few faded, water-damaged books with pages so brittle they crumble at the edges, and a small, tarnished metal cup. Violet barely glances at them, focusing instead on the more immediate need. She gathers up a blanket first, folding it as best as she can within the limited space.

Next, she picks up a few cans of food and a bottle of water. The cans are dusty and dented but still sealed. She shoves them into the backpack with the blanket, not bothering to check the expiration dates.

As she stands, the backpack begins to sag under the weight, its old leather straps creaking slightly. She adjusts it, hoisting it onto her shoulders, trying to balance the load. The rustling of the supplies and the clink of the cans echo softly in the tunnel, the sound swallowed by silence.

With the backpack now packed, she takes one last look at the stash. The books, their pages too worn and water-stained to be of any use, are left behind.

As Violet turns to retrace her steps towards the entrance of the tunnel, she brushes off a layer of damp dust from her hair. The small particles cling to her fingers, and a hint of moisture makes her skin feel sticky. She pulls her face mask up to cover her mouth and nose, trying to shield herself from the unsettling mix of grime and humidity.

She edges closer to the rock slab, her breath catching in her throat. Peering through the narrow opening, her eyes widen as she takes in the sight outside.

The dull gray sky has become even more muted, the colors fading into a gloomy palette of whites and grays. The ruins seem to blur and soften at the edges, swallowed by the mist.

The fog is back.

CHAPTER 7

VIOLET SPRINTS TOWARDS the tunnel's entrance. The tunnel narrows ahead, the dim light barely guiding her steps. The weight on her back pulls her down, each step heavier than the last. She grits her teeth as she stumbles on the uneven ground.

The backpack. It's slowing her down.

Without second thought, she unclasps the straps and lets it drop. The thud echoes, but she doesn't look back. Her hands are already on the stone, fingers digging into the rough surface as she pushes with all her strength. The stone grinds against the ground, resisting her efforts.

Almost there.

"Wait!"

Violet freezes, the stone more than halfway closed. Her heart pounds against her ribs, shivers creeping up her spine. The rumors—they say fog monsters can imitate voices.

Her hands tighten on the stone, muscles tense, eager to slam it shut.

What do I do?

It could be a trick.

It could be —

A hand shoots in from the white cast of the outside, stopping the stone from closing all the way. The fingers are small, trembling. Violet gets a flash of fire orange hair through the gap — the twins.

She hesitates at first, but then, in a split second, pulls the stone back just enough for them to squeeze through

They both collapse onto the cold, hard ground of the tunnel, chests heaving. Elliot doubles over, a harsh cough rattling through his body. Ellie, crouches beside him, lightly patting his back.

"Do you have any water?" Ellie's voice is hoarse, desperate.

Violet's gaze flicks to the spot where she dropped the backpack. She nods once, and without a word, turns and retraces her steps.

She grabs the bag and hurries back. Dropping to her knees beside them, she yanks out a water bottle, the plastic slightly slimy and sticky where the label used to be. She hands it to Elliot, her eyes fixed on the seal.

Please, let it be good.

The cap cracks open with a sharp pop as Elliot twists it. Relief washes over Violet, the tension in her shoulders easing as Elliot lifts the bottle to his lips. He drinks in big gulps, each one punctuated by harsh coughs that gradually soften and space out until they stop.

He pushes the bottle away towards his sister as he wipes his mouth with the back of his free hand.

Ellie takes the bottle from him and wipes the opening with the hem of her shirt. She takes nothing but a small sip, cleaning it again before closing it and handing it back to Violet still half full. "Thank you," she says.

Violet blinks rapidly, her gaze shifting between the bottle and Ellie. "Wait, I thought you guys were..."

"Deaf?" Ellie finishes the sentence for her, a small, knowing smile tugging at her lips. Violet nods. "Elliot is deaf. I'm not," Ellie explains. "But since we're twins and we both use sign language when we're together, people kind of assume."

"I see..." Violet mutters, lowering her gaze as her cheeks flush with warmth.

I'm an idiot.

So embarrassing.

Elliot coughs again, a deep, rasping sound that seems to scrape the inside of his throat. Ellie immediately shifts her focus back to him, her hand moving in comforting circles on his back. She signs something with one hand, her other arm wrapping around his shoulders.

Violet guides them deeper into the tunnel, back to where she had discovered the supplies. She rummages through the pile, pulling out a couple of sleeping bags, then spreads them out on the stone floor. Elliot sinks onto the makeshift bed, his body heavy with exhaustion. Ellie reaches into his backpack, retrieving a small battery lamp that casts a pale glow over the small space. As she brushes the back of her hand against his forehead, her brow furrows, her fingers lingering on his skin.

"He's burning up," Ellie murmurs, tucking the blanket around him with care. "You need to rest," she adds, her voice as soft as her hands as she signs the words to her brother.

Elliot barely nods, his eyes already half-closed.

Violet hesitates, questions hanging on her lips. Finally, she breaks the silence, and she finds herself whispering even though Elliot can't hear her. "What happened?"

Ellie glances up, her lips pressing into a slight pout. Her gaze shifts back to Elliot, her fingers threading gently through his damp, sweaty hair as she speaks. "He inhaled too much of the fog today. We thought we could outrun it, but... he started coughing so hard, couldn't catch his breath."

Violet's heart sinks. The fog. The rumors hadn't done it justice—the stories about what it could do to people who lingered for too long. She swallows hard.

"Is there anything we can do?" Violet asks.

"There is no medicine here." Ellie shakes her head slowly. "All we can do is keep him warm and hope it goes away."

Violet leans in closer, her voice barely above a whisper. "Have you seen them? The monsters?"

Ellie's face drains of color, her hands tremble slightly as she grips the edge of the blanket covering Elliot. "I've seen them," she says, her voice hollow. "We… we found a couple of bodies. They were torn apart like nothing I've ever seen. We couldn't even bring ourselves to look at their faces, to see if… if we knew them." Her eyes dart to the shadows around them, as if expecting one of the creatures to emerge at any moment. "Have you…?" Ellie asks.

Violet's stomach churns, the words digging into her like a knife. Her mind races, images of what Ellie might have seen flashing through her thoughts. The image of Lorenzo's face, lifeless and unrecognizable, the memory clawing its way out from where she's buried it. She can still see the blood, feel the coldness of his skin as she turned him over.

Her voice wavers as she replies, "No, I haven't seen them. Not yet." But she's seen the aftermath. She's seen what they leave behind. "Lorenzo's dead. I found him—his body. I… I don't know what happened. He was just there, like he'd been… beaten to death." The memory claws at her, and she chokes on the guilt lodged in her throat. "It was my idea to keep watch. I thought it would keep us safe. But now… he's dead because of me."

"What's your name?" Ellie interrupts.

Violet takes a deep breath. "Violet."

"Ah, so you're Violet." Ellie's gaze softens, and she shifts closer to her, placing a comforting hand on her shoulder. "Violet, listen to me," she says gently. "It's not your fault. We all have to make choices in this place, and sometimes they don't turn out the way we hope. Aiden's group was on guard too, and no one died. It was just… an unfortunate accident."

Violet's shoulders slump, the weight of Ellie's words a small comfort amidst her guilt. Her eyes glisten, but she fights the tears back, the pain still pressing against her chest. "But I should have done more. I should have—"

"No," Ellie interrupts again. "You did what you thought was right. Sometimes, that's all we can do. You couldn't have known. It's not your fault. We're all just trying to survive here."

Violet nods, her breath catching as she tries to steady herself. She swallows hard, and her stomach growls, a low, persistent rumble that seems to echo through the tunnel. She frowns, her cheeks flushing as the sound seems to amplify her hunger.

Ellie glances at her with a sympathetic smile, a soft giggle escaping as she covers her mouth. "I agree. Eating would be an amazing idea," she says, her eyes crinkling at the corners.

Violet's fingers fumble through the cans, their labels worn and useless. She picks one at random. With a firm grip, she drives her knife into the lid, working it around the edge until the metal gives way, leaving a jagged, uneven opening.

Ellie reaches into her crossbody bag and pulls out a small, silver device that resembles a compact disc. With a click, it emits a soft hum. "It's designed to keep drinks warm," Ellie says, placing the heater carefully beneath the can. "But it should do the trick, at least enough to make this a bit more edible."

The can's contents begin to bubble slightly, the surface shimmering with a greasy sheen. Violet watches as the steam curls up into the dim light, but instead of a savory aroma, a rank, sour odor wafts through the air. The food inside looks slimy, an unappealing mix of textures that cling to the sides of the can. Yet, as her stomach growls louder, the hunger gnawing at her insides distorts the scent, making it strangely inviting. Her mouth waters despite the queasiness twisting in her gut.

Ellie rummages through the supply pile and finds a small sachet of mismatched metal spoons and forks. She hands one to Violet, and they settle down on the cold ground, sitting cross-legged on the blankets they didn't use for Elliot. Ellie dips her spoon into the can first, scooping up a glob of thick, lumpy stew. The texture is off—slimy and unappealing, with chunks that seem more like congealed fat than meat. The smell is rancid, a sour tang mingling with an underlying mustiness.

Violet follows suit, the metallic taste of the can mixing with the stew's off-putting flavor. It's disgusting, but it's food, and as each spoonful goes down, they push past the nausea, focusing only on the desperate need to fill their stomachs.

Elliot coughs, each sound a harsh rasp as he struggles to swallow the stew. His face flushes with effort, and he tilts his head back, trying to ease the burning in his throat.

"Oh Elliot," she says, her voice dry but her hands moving with practiced precision as she signs. "If only you could hear how awful your coughs sound."

Violet stifles a small giggle, the sound escaping despite her efforts to contain it—but her laugh quickly fades. She looks down at the leftover stew in the can, stirring it absently. "I'm trying to find a way to get out of here. Do you know if there's an exit?"

Ellie puts down her spoon, cleaning the corner of her mouth with her thumb. "Out of the Paracosm?" Violet nods. "Well, some of us try to fight the monsters. Some of us are just trying to survive. No matter what you choose to do, staying alive is the most important part. The High Council will come get us after a week."

Violet's eyes widen. "People have survived this thing?"

Ellie shrugs. "Not a lot. It's rare. But the ones who do survive are never the same."

Violet's brow furrows. "I can't believe the Council would make their own people go through this."

Ellie's eyes, though tired, hold a glint at the mention of the High Council. "It's an honor, you know. What if we find a way to kill the monsters or keep them away? I will gladly die here if that means my family and future generations have a chance of living in peace."

Violet's gaze drops to the empty can between them, its last traces of steam blending with the musty air. She thinks of the villagers, the sacrifices she's made for them, and the burden of her choices that led her to be here right now. "I understand," she says, her voice low. "I'd do the same."

Ellie's expression softens, her lips curving into a genuine smile. "Well, you are doing the same." Her hand rests gently on Violet's arm. "You're here. You're one of us."

They chat for a while, their voices mingling with the faint hum of the heater. The warmth of the stew seems to revive Elliot, who now sits up more energetically despite his lingering fever.

Violet's gaze drifts toward the entrance. "I'm not sure how we'll know when the fog's gone," she murmurs, her eyes scanning the tunnel. "It's not like we can stay here forever."

Ellie adjusts her position, her hands moving, accompanying her words. "We have a timer." She gestures to her wrist as she signs. "Aiden figured out a pattern. The fog comes in cycles—an hour every two hours."

Violet absorbs this new information, her thoughts racing. The pattern, if accurate, could be their key to surviving, or even running away.

Elliot's hands move with both sharp and fluid gestures, a stream of signs flowing between him and Ellie. Violet watches, her gaze fixed on Ellie, waiting for her to translate.

"He wants to know if you've explored the entire tunnel."

"Oh, no I haven't." Violet shakes her head. "I know a couple of paths are blocked, but not all of them."

Elliot nods.

Violet frowns.

Is she not going to translate what I said?

Ellie smiles, as if she could read her mind. "Oh, don't worry," she says, signing along with her words. "He can read your lips."

They share one more can of food and take a long drink of water. With their hunger momentarily satiated, they gather themselves and press onward to explore the labyrinth of tunnels.

The air grows colder and denser as they move, carrying the earthy scent of old stone. The tunnel narrows and twists, the uneven floor occasionally giving way to deep puddles.

Ellie leads the way, her light revealing sporadic hints of old and faded drawings on the walls—sketches of monsters, crude and frightening.

They come across a small side passage that strays off from the main tunnel. The passage is barely wide enough for one person to squeeze through, but they all manage their way in. The light from their lamp flickers as they step inside, revealing a large, round cavern.

The space is cluttered with remnants of what looks to have been a camping site. Rotted, moldy blankets lie strewn across the cold ground, their colors muted and indistinct. An old, tattered tent stands against one wall, its fabric sagging and torn. There's clutter everywhere—empty rusted cans with faded labels, broken cookware, and the remains of a small, neglected fire pit, its ashes turned to dust.

Violet's eyes are drawn to a pile of dusty, yellowed papers and brittle, leather-bound diaries haphazardly stacked beside the remnants of a crumbling backpack. She kneels to inspect them. The musty smell of decay wafts up as she opens one of the diaries.

The pages are filled with cramped words, the ink smeared and fading in places. The entries are in a foreign language, but the handwriting is so messy that most of it would be barely legible anyway.

"St. Marrow has been monolingual for a long time," Ellie says, crouching beside Violet, her light falling over the diaries. "These must be from decades ago."

Elliot snaps his fingers, drawing Ellie and Violet's attention. In one hand, he clutches a crumpled piece of paper, while several others lie scattered at his feet. He signs something, then tosses the paper back to the ground with a flick of his wrist.

Ellie turns to Violet. "He says these papers look more recent." she explains.

Violet bends down and carefully picks up one of the crumpled sheets. The paper feels fragile between her fingers, as if it might disintegrate with too much pressure. Slowly, she unfolds it, revealing the faded ink scrawled across the page.

They're here again. I see them everywhere. I need to stop breathing. I need to hold it in. Hold it — just a little longer. They hate it. It makes them weak. But I can't. I'm drowning. Please, please make it stop. I tried holding my breath. I tried so hard. I'll have to gasp for air soon. It's over for me. It's over.

A chill creeps up Violet's spine as she reads, the jagged lines of faded black pulling her into the writer's frantic state. She becomes more aware of the dampness in the air clinging to her skin, as if the fear engraved into the paper is alive, crawling up her arms.

Ellie's voice breaks through her rising panic, pulling her back. "Violet, look at this."

Violet blinks, her focus shifting to Ellie, who is holding out another piece of paper. This one is less crumpled, but still worn at the edges. The words are more carefully written, the handwriting steady, but hurried.

"It looks like a page from a diary," Ellie says.

Day 1

Julia is gone. My dear Julia, taken by this cursed place.
We couldn't save her. The miner boys and I are digging a tunnel.
We'll bury her there, away from the fog.

Day 3

It's just Vincent and me now.
The tunnel seems safe—the fog doesn't reach us here.
I pray it stays that way.

Day 5

We're both falling ill.
The Paracosm ends in two days.
The High Council will come for us, they'll save us.
I hope Vincent makes it until then.

Day 6

Vincent didn't make it.
I woke to find him cold, lifeless.
Rest easy, my friend.
I'll return your ring to your family, I swear it.

Day 7

I hear soldiers outside.
They've been here for hours, collecting dead bodies, one by one.
They don't sound scared or cautious of the monsters.
My fever is getting worse.

Day 10

The soldiers are gone.
The fog hasn't returned since they left.
What did they do?

Day 13

My rations are nearly gone.
I can feel myself withering away.
I don't know how much longer I have.

Violet's eyes dart across the page, the words blurring together as she tries to make sense of them. The first entries are haunting enough, but it's the later ones that send her mind spiraling.

The soldiers are gone. The fog hasn't returned since they left.

She reads the sentence over and over, her brow furrowing. What does it mean? The fog just... stopped? How could that be? The fog had seemed relentless, an unstoppable force. The idea that it could simply vanish, tied somehow to the presence of these soldiers, makes no sense. She glances up at Ellie.

"The fog stopped? Is that even possible?" Violet says.

Ellie, reading over her shoulder, bites her lip. "I don't know. Aiden and Conrad kept tabs on it the whole night. There is a pattern for sure, but it never fully stopped."

As if on cue, a soft beep and vibration from Elliot's pocket watch cut through the thick silence. Both girls glance at him, and he holds up the watch, nodding to confirm what they all know — the fog is gone, at least for the next two hours.

Violet pushes the diary page into Ellie's hand. "I'm going outside," she says.

CHAPTER 8

VIOLET STORMS TOWARDS the entrance of the tunnel, each step a harsh stomp against the ground. Ellie hurries after her. "Violet, wait!" she pleads, reaching out as if she could physically pull her back. "Don't do this. It's not safe."

Violet doesn't stop. "You said it yourself. There's a pattern. The fog is gone," she says, still closing the distance between her and the outside.

Ellie's breath hitches as she struggles to keep up with her pace. "But what if the pattern is wrong? What if something's changed?"

"What if it hasn't?" Violet shoots back.

"Those writings gave me a bad feeling, Violet. They talked about a fever, just like my brother's, and the fog... I don't know what to think anymore."

Violet slows just enough to glance over her shoulder, her expression softening for a fleeting moment. "I'm sorry," she says.

As soon as the apology escapes her mouth, a memory comes back to her, dragging her back to the last time she'd spoken those exact words—to Ethan, before she left the village. The image of his face, the pain in his eyes, rushes back to her with startling clarity. Her heart clenches with the reminder of why she needs to leave this place.

Violet stands before the stone barrier. She takes a deep breath, the air inside the tunnel stale and cold against her lungs. Her fingers curl around the rough edge of the rock, the texture gritty and cool under her touch.

She hesitates for just a second, her thoughts racing. What if Ellie's right? What if the pattern has changed, if the fog is still out there?

She takes a deep breath once more before pushing the rock aside. The sound of grinding stone echoes in the tunnel, loud and grating, as the barrier slowly gives way. A sliver of light slices through the darkness, growing wider and brighter as the rock shifts.

Violet squints as the outside world is revealed, her eyes struggling to adjust to the sudden brightness after so long in the dim, shadowy tunnel. The light is harsh, almost blinding, and she blinks rapidly, her vision a blur of white and gray. Her senses flinch from the harsh contrast, the cool dampness of the tunnel giving way to the dry, crisp air of the outside.

As her eyes gradually adjust, shapes and colors start to come into focus—the pale gray sky overhead, the crumbling, rocky ruins. Everything is quiet. Nothing stirs—not a leaf, not a shadow.

Violet's boots crunch softly on the gravel as she lets her gaze drift across the empty space, searching for any sign of movement, any indication that the monsters had been around. But there's nothing—no footprints, no creatures, no trace of the chaos that had gripped the Paracosm mere hours ago.

The soldiers are gone. The fog hasn't returned since they left.

The phrase from the diary echoes in her mind, refusing to settle. She tries to piece together its meaning, turning the words over and over, hoping to find clarity in the repetition. But the more she thinks about it, the less sense it makes.

The fog hasn't returned since they left.

Her thoughts spiral. Could the fog have been connected to the soldiers, tied to their presence? No. It can't be. The fog is everywhere, enclosing St. Marrow, trapping everyone inside.

She paces the area, careful not to stray too far from the tunnel's entrance. Each step stirs up clouds of dust and sand from the crumbling ruins, particles swirling around her. The gritty air bites at her throat, leaving it raw and scratchy. She pulls her face mask up, securing it over her mouth and nose, the fabric pressing tight against her skin as she breathes in the filtered air.

Violet's eyes narrow as she squints into the distance, struggling to make out a figure emerging from the shadowy edge of the forest.

She cups her hands over the mask, shouting, "Hello? Are you okay?"

No response.

Violet takes a cautious step closer, her eyes straining to make out more details. The person wears thick, heavy gloves and a gas mask that obscures their face.

"Do you need help? We found shelter!" Violet shouts again.

No response.

For a moment, the figure stands still. Then, without a word, they bolt, their silhouette darting along the edge where the forest meets the ruins.

Violet's heart pounds in her chest as she follows the figure's erratic, panicked movements. She runs after them, her first steps hesitant, but she quickens her pace, the ground beneath her blurring as she transitions into a full sprint.

"Wait! I just want to help!" Violet's voice cracks through the air, but the figure doesn't slow. Instead, it bolts faster, disappearing around a corner of the ruins.

Violet skids to a halt, her breath coming in sharp, uneven gasps. She swipes at her forehead, expecting some sweat but feeling an unexpected amount of dampness. Her fingers come away wet, and her eyes dart upward. The sky remains a relentless shade of gray.

Then, shifting her gaze to the forest's edge, she sees it: the top of the trees becoming increasingly indistinct, their outlines dissolving into a gloomy haze.

The fog is back.

What?

It can't be.

It hasn't even been half an hour.

She whirls around, sprinting towards the tunnel, her legs pumping in frantic rhythm. The fog thickens, curling around her ankles, the ground shifting beneath her feet.

Her vision blurs, the crumbling structures fading into a single white cloud. Panic tightens her chest as the fog swallows the path ahead, the once-clear route to the tunnel now a swirling void. She pushes herself harder, ignoring the stitch in her side, the cold dampness seeping through her clothes. She needs to reach the tunnel before the fog makes it impossible to find her way back.

Faster.

Run faster.

She fumbles with her mask, adjusting the straps with shaking fingers, ensuring it's tightly sealed against her face. Visibility shrinks with every passing second. Distorted clumps of shadows loom and vanish as the fog curls and twists, playing tricks on her eyes.

Violet's fingers close around the jagged edges of the rock, her palms slick with sweat and trembling slightly. Her breath comes in short, sharp bursts, and the fog presses heavily against her, making the air feel like it's closing in.

I did it.

I'm here.

As she braces herself to shove the rock aside, a faint, desperate cry cuts through the fog.

"Help!"

The sound is distant, but it is unmistakably a plea for help. Violet freezes, her heart pounding against her ribs. The fog seems to part momentarily, allowing the sound to reach her, and she hears it again—a strained, muffled voice, pleading, reaching out.

"Help!"

The choice hangs heavily in the air. Her instinct is to rush into the tunnel, to escape the fog and find safety. Yet, the desperate cry for help tugs at her heart, pulling her in the direction of the voice.

Violet glances back towards the ruins, the hazy shapes and shadows barely noticeable in the thick mist. Every second feels like an eternity. Violet's fingers tighten around the rock, her muscles straining with the effort.

She turns away from the tunnel's entrance, leaving the safety of it behind. The fog presses around her, a relentless, shifting force that grows thicker with every step. Her breath catches in her throat, and her mask feels suffocating as she pushes forward.

The screams become louder, more urgent. Violet squints through the thick, swirling mists, her eyes straining to pick out shapes, something, anything.

And then, through the fog, she sees *him*.

Aiden stumbles into view, wavering as he falls heavily to the ground. His movements are frantic, almost animalistic. He twists around, struggling against nothing, his eyes wide with terror as he scrambles backwards, dragging himself away.

"Help!" he croaks, his voice raspy and tired. "Please, help!"

Aiden writhes on the ground, his movements frantic and erratic. The fog is thick and swirling, obscuring the details, but she can clearly see Aiden's silhouette. His body jerks violently, as if he's being struck by unseen forces. His face, though mostly covered by the fog, is twisted in fear, his eyes wide and open.

He claws at the air, and every few seconds, he stops to glance over his shoulder, his face contorted in terror. His breaths come in loud, ragged bursts, and he's mumbling something incoherently, slurring his words. Violet's heart races as she tries to make sense of the scene before her.

There's nothing.

Nothing—just a dense, oppressive veil of fog that blurs the world. There are no monsters, nobody, only Aiden's panicked responses. She sees him fall to his knees, then drag himself backwards, his hands scraping against the ground. The effort seems to exhaust him, his movements becoming weaker and more desperate with each passing moment.

Violet charges through the fog. She pushes through the dense whiteness until Aiden's outline becomes more distinct. His body is slumped on the ground, trembling uncontrollably.

She reaches for him, her hands grasping his shoulders firmly. Aiden flinches, squinting his eyes tightly shut, and pushes her away with a frantic shove. "Aiden stop, it's just me."

He blinks rapidly, his gaze darting around as if he's searching for something. "Run… away. Save yourself. Why are you here?" His voice is strained, hoarse.

Violet pulls him up, struggling against his dead weight as she slips her arm around his shoulders, trying to steady him. "You need to come with me. We have shelter. It's safe." Her voice is firm, though she can still feel the tremor in it. She tugs at him gently, trying to guide him up.

Aiden's eyes lock onto hers. He hesitates, the terror in his stare mingling with confusion. "Shelter?" he repeats, his voice wavering. "But…the monsters…"

"Yes, shelter!" Violet says urgently, her grip steady as she supports him. "The fog is getting worse. We need to move now."

With a last glance over his shoulder, Aiden nods weakly. Violet supports him as they walk, their first steps slow. She leads him carefully through the thickening fog, her visibility shrinking as they move.

We're not gonna make it.

Not like this.

"We need to run," Violet says as she grips Aiden's hand tightly, her fingers intertwining with his. His grip is weak, but he still clings to her. They sprint together, the fog swirling around them in thick waves.

She guides him, their steps unsteady on the uneven ground. Violet's other hand clutches the edge of her mask, pulling it tightly over her face to filter out the fog as best as she can.

Finally, through a thick layer of white, emerges the outline of the crumbled house. The entrance to the tunnel is just ahead. Aiden's footsteps falter, but she grips his hand tighter, urging him forward.

"Almost there," Violet calls out, her voice muffled by her mask.

With one last burst of effort, they reach the entrance. Violet stumbles slightly as she pushes against the heavy rock blocking the tunnel, her hands fumbling to open it.

The rock shifts as the entrance begins to reveal itself. She pushes Aiden through the gap, guiding him inside with the last of her strength.

They collapse inside, Violet immediately turning to close the door behind them with an echoing thud. She leans against the wall, her breath coming in ragged gasps as she pulls down her mask. She glances at Aiden, who slumps to the ground.

"We're safe," Violet whispers, her voice trembling as she sinks down beside him.

Ellie and Elliot's hurried footsteps echo off the stone walls. Ellie's eyes widen as she sees Aiden's disheveled state, her breath catching in her throat.

Aiden's gaze remains unfocused, distant. He flinches violently at every sound, every movement, his body curling into itself. The tension in his shoulders is palpable, and he mutters incoherently, the words a mix of panic and confusion. "I saw them…I did…" His once steady hands are now shaking uncontrollably, gripping at the edge of his clothes.

Elliot moves swiftly to Aiden's side, crouching down. His hands, though gentle, are firm as he tries to ground Aiden, offering silent support.

Ellie reaches out, her hand resting lightly on Violet's shoulder as she watches Aiden's distress unfold. Her voice trembles slightly as she asks, "What happened?"

Violet, still catching her breath, replies, "The fog came back."

Ellie's brow furrows. "But it wasn't supposed to come back for more than an hour. The pattern…"

"The pattern is wrong." Violet shakes her head, her gaze still fixed on Aiden. "…or the fog is changing."

Aiden, his eyes wide, turns to them. He grabs Violet's arm with a shaky grip, his voice trembling. "Thank you… for saving me. I didn't think I'd make it."

Violet hesitates, her gaze flicking between Aiden and his touch. She places her hand gently over his, her voice soft. "Aiden…" She pauses, weighing her words. "There was nothing there."

"What do you mean, nothing? I saw it. It was right there. It was attacking *me*." He yanks his hand away from hers, rising to his feet. "It almost attacked *you*. How can you say there was nothing?"

Violet's brow creases as she recalls the scene. "I only saw you crawling on the ground, screaming," she says. "There was nothing around you, nothing attacking you. And look at you—not even a scratch."

Aiden stumbles back a step, his hand instinctively moving to his chest as if searching for wounds that don't exist. His breath quickens, chest heaving as he tries to process her words. "No," he whispers, almost to himself, shaking his head. "No, I felt it. I saw it!" His voice rises, cracking with desperation.

Violet stands, her eyes locking with Aiden's. "I swear, Aiden, there was nothing there," she says. "Just you, and the fog. I think… you were hallucinating."

Aiden's face drains of color. He wraps his arms around his torso, as if trying to hold himself together. "I—I don't—" His voice falters, barely more than a whisper. "No, it can't be…" He shudders. "It was right there…"

Ellie, standing just a few steps away, looks between them. Her gaze flicks from Violet, to Aiden, to the rock that leads outside, then back again. "But… how come you didn't see anything, Violet?" she asks. "You were in the fog too."

Elliot catches Ellie's attention with a quick movement, his hands signing something that makes her eyes widen. She gasps, raising her hands to her mouth as she stares at Violet.

"What did he say?" Aiden asks, still on edge.

Ellie lowers her hands, her eyes still locked on Violet. "Your mask," she says, pointing at Violet's neck with her index finger.

"The mask…" Aiden repeats the word almost under his breath.

"The fog is dense, thicker than dust," Ellie says. "Your mask was blocking it for sure."

Violet's heart skips a beat. The words hang in the air, and everything starts to unravel inside her mind. The notes in the cavern, scrawled in desperate, shaking handwriting— *I need to stop breathing. I need to hold it in.* It all clicks.

Her breath quickens, each inhalation sharper than the last. The fog isn't hiding the monsters—it is the monster. A shiver crawls down her spine. The fever, the hallucinations—

people weren't just dying—they were being driven mad, consumed from the inside out.

Her thoughts spiral, racing through every encounter, every story she'd heard. The screams, the terror, the things they saw, her parents—none of it was real. At least, not in the way they thought. The fog isn't some supernatural force bringing nightmares to life. The fog is poisoning them.

Violet's knees feel weak, a nauseating dread curling in her stomach. Instinctively, she reaches up, clutching the black face mask that dangles around her neck, the thin fabric now feeling like the only thing standing between her and the madness that nearly claimed Aiden.

Ellie's arm intertwines with hers, grounding her, pulling her back from the edge of panic.

"Let's go back to the campsite," Ellie says softly. Ellie's gentle tug urges Violet forward, her feet moving almost mechanically as they leave the entrance to the tunnel behind.

"Wait..." Violet halts abruptly, her breath catching in her throat. "But... Lorenzo's body..."

Aiden's face turns pale as he looks at Violet. "Lorenzo's dead?"

"Violet found his body," Ellie replies, her eyes drifting to the ground between them.

"His head..." Violet's mind flashes back to the gruesome scene of Lorenzo's lifeless form sprawled on the rock, his head a bloody mess of crushed flesh and shattered bone. "...was smashed against a rock." The memory of the grotesque sight churns her stomach.

"If the fog makes you hallucinate," Aiden says slowly, his voice low and hoarse, "it's very possible that he just... banged his head against the rock multiple times."

Ellie's face contorts in disgust, and she chokes back a gag. Violet can feel the bile rising in her own throat, every muscle in her body straining to maintain composure.

Elliot signs, his fingers moving with precision, but with slow and short movements. Ellie watches him, her eyes growing sadder with each gesture. "I agree," she says softly. "I feel bad for anyone lost out there in the fog. If only they knew the monsters aren't real."

Ellie's words force Violet's thoughts to race back to the fleeting glimpse she had of the person in the gas mask moving through the ruins. It had seemed so out of place then, but now it makes a grim sort of sense.

That person…

They know something.

"There was someone else outside," Violet tells the group. "They were wearing a gas mask and gloves. I saw them just before the fog came back."

Ellie scratches the back of her head, her gaze shifting to the ground. "Maybe it was also a hallucination," she suggests.

Aiden's expression darkens, his gaze locking with Violet's. "No," he says firmly. "I saw them too."

CHAPTER 9

DURING THE SAFE hours of the day, Violet ventures outside several times, the fabric of her mask secured tightly over her nose and mouth. She moves cautiously among the decaying structures, eyes scanning the horizon for any sign of the person wearing a gas mask.

I need to find them.

The ruins stand silent and empty, their broken forms casting jagged silhouettes against the never changing gray sky.

On her last trip outside, as the light dips low and paints the sky with muted grays, Violet sits atop a crumbled wall. She waits, listening intently to the whispers of the wind and the distant rustle of leaves.

Violet stands, glancing back one last time, sweeping over the ruins. With a deep sigh, she turns and retraces her steps, her boots crunching softly over the gravel. The journey back to the tunnel feels longer in the growing darkness, each step heavy with the weight of her fruitless search. She reaches the entrance of the tunnel, and slips inside. The cool, damp air of the cavern envelops her as she removes her mask and stores it carefully on the inside pocket of her jacket.

Ellie, who had been sitting cross-legged on the floor, rises slowly as Violet steps deeper into the tunnel. The faint glow of the lantern she carries casts a warm light on her tired face, highlighting the lines of concern across her features.

"Find anything?" Ellie asks.

Violet shakes her head, her shoulders slumping. "No sign of them," she replies.

"It's been quiet today. Maybe they've gone further away."

Violet nods. "Or maybe they're hiding," she says, hands firm on both of her hips. "I have this weird feeling that I'm missing something…something important."

Ellie steps closer, placing a reassuring hand on Violet's shoulder. "You've done everything you can for now."

"Thank you."

"Also," Ellie says as they walk back to the cavern camp, "before we settle down for the night, I have an idea."

"What idea?"

Ellie reaches into her bag and pulls out a small metal tin. "Since you're the only one with a mask, I think we should make some for the rest of us." She opens the lid to reveal a small, basic sewing kit. "Do you know how?"

Violet nods. "I'll give it a go."

As soon as they reach the camp, Violet gathers any useful materials she can find. There are various scraps and old pieces of cloth inside the tents and old backpacks. The fabrics vary in thickness and texture—some are remnants of old uniforms, while others are heavier materials that might offer additional protection.

Sitting down with the sewing kit, Violet spreads out the fabrics and begins to work. The sewing kit is simple but functional, and Violet's fingers move with practiced ease as she cuts and stitches the pieces together. The masks take shape, each one a patchwork of different fabrics and colors.

Ellie helps as much as she can, handing Violet materials and offering occasional guidance. Aiden and Elliot, meanwhile, watch them in silence.

As Violet finishes the last mask, she examines them with a nod of approval. They aren't perfect, but they're an improvement over nothing. She hands them out one by one.

"These should do," Violet says. "We'll test them tomorrow when we go out."

Ellie smiles. "Thanks, Violet. You're an angel."

For the rest of the day, they check every corner of the underground passages and nearby structures, searching desperately for answers, for any sort of information. Dusty journals and crumpled notes litter the floors of multiple abandoned camps, remnants of those who came before them. Violet kneels beside a scattered pile of papers, her fingers tracing the faded ink on a torn page.

The whispers are growing louder. I see shapes in the fog, but when I reach out, there's nothing. Am I losing myself to this place?

She sets it aside and picks up another, this time a letter, its paper wrinkled and brittle beneath her touch.

If anyone ever finds this note,
Please, remember me. I don't want to be just another body left to rot in the fog.
The fever's getting worse. I can feel it burning me up from the inside, boiling my blood, making it hard to think, hard to breathe. I know what's coming. I've seen what happens to others, how they start to cough up blood, how their skin turns that awful gray.
I thought maybe, just maybe, I could make it further than them, that I could find some way out. But I know that's not going to happen. My legs won't carry me much longer, and my hands shake too much to even hold this pen steady.

Please, if you find this—whoever you are—know that I fought as long as I could. I didn't want to go like this, alone in the dark, with no one to even say goodbye to.

Tell someone I was here. Tell someone I tried.

Tell them my name is—

The name has been smeared away, illegible.

Each new discovery mirrors the last, a chorus of fear and confusion from old times— not that much has changed in the Paracosm.

The atmosphere grows tenser with each passing hour. Elliot lies curled under a thin blanket, his face flushed and damp with sweat. His breaths come in shallow, uneven patterns, each one a struggle.

Ellie sits beside him, brushing strands of hair away from his forehead. The rise in his temperature throughout the day has been relentless, and now, in the stillness of night, his condition appears to be worse.

Violet settles across from them, her back against the cold stone wall. The chill seeps through her clothes, but she hardly notices. She watches as Ellie adjusts the blanket around her brother.

"I'm scared," Ellie says, her voice barely above a whisper. "The notes… the people… how they didn't survive the fever. I can't stop thinking about it."

Violet's eyes drift to the scattered notes beside them, the words of strangers now entwined with their own reality. "It explains a lot," Violet says, taking a slow deep breath. "Back in my village, people get fevers all the time. Even the children. We're right on the edge of the fog, and we never understood why this sickness was so common. I guess we just assumed malnourishment was to blame."

"I just hope he'll be ok," Ellie murmurs. "I don't know what I'd do without him."

A heavy pause settles between them, filled only by the soft rustle of fabric and labored breaths as Elliot shifts, turning and tossing under his blanket.

"We'll keep an eye on him tonight," Violet says. "Make sure he stays as comfortable as possible."

Ellie's lips curl into a small, weary smile, her eyes glowing. "I appreciate it. Thank you."

The lantern's light flickers, casting dancing shadows that play across the rough surfaces surrounding them. The batteries must be running low, but not so low that they need to be changed.

As the minutes tick by, Violet's gaze drifts upward, following the contours of the tunnel ceiling where cracks spread out across the stone. The rhythmic sounds echo around her — the raspy inhale and exhale of Elliot's breathing, the soft rustle of Ellie adjusting her own sleeping bag, the distant, almost imperceptible sigh of the wind outside.

Her thoughts wander back to the figure in the gas mask, the unanswered questions gnawing at the edges of her mind. Who are they? How long have they been here? What do they know? The unknowns twist inside her, fueling a feeling of restlessness that keeps sleep at bay.

I have to find them.

Pulling her knees to her chest, Violet wraps her arms around herself, seeking some warmth and comfort in her own embrace. Aiden works beside her, spreading out his sleeping bag on the cold, uneven ground.

"Looks like we're set," Aiden says, his voice quiet. He glances over at Violet, who nods absently, her mind elsewhere.

She unrolls her own sleeping bag next to his, the material crackling as she tries to smooth it out. The fabric feels thin and plasticky under her fingers, cold and slightly stiff, offering little to no comfort as she slips inside — but it's better than the floor.

Aiden settles down beside her, their shoulders almost touching, though neither acknowledges it.

As the moments stretch on, Violet's eyes remain open, still tracing the jagged cracks in the stone wall next to her. She shifts, trying to find a position where the uneven ground doesn't press too hard on her hip or dig into her shoulder.

"Can't sleep either?"

Violet freezes at the sound of Aiden's voice, her breath catching as she stops her fidgeting. She closes her eyes, pretending to be asleep. The darkness around them feels thick, but even without sight, she can feel his gaze on her.

"I know you're awake," he says, clearly smirking through his words.

She opens her eyes, the ruse falling apart under his persistence. "Go to sleep," she mutters, keeping her voice low to avoid disturbing Ellie and Elliot.

"What? Don't be shy." He lets out a small chuckle. "The night's young, and it's normal for a little mouse to be more active at night."

She turns her head, just enough to catch the faint outline of his profile in the dim light of the now almost dead lantern. "Stop calling me that," she warns him, though the edge in her tone lacks real anger.

"Why?" he replies, unfazed. "It's fitting, don't you think? You're quiet, sneaky… short."

Violet rolls her eyes, even though he can't see it. "And you're a fox, I suppose?"

"Maybe," he says, his voice dropping to a more serious note. "But even foxes need sleep."

She huffs, a small, reluctant laugh escaping from her. "Then go to sleep, Aiden."

For the following moments, there's only the sound of their breathing and the quiet murmur of the night. Violet shifts again, settling deeper into her sleeping bag, the banter between them distracting her just enough to push the swirling thoughts to the back of her mind.

Aiden's voice cuts through the silence again, softer this time. "We'll figure this out. I know we will." Violet doesn't respond, but his words linger. Somehow, she believes him.

Violet lies there for a moment, staring into the darkness. Then quietly, she shifts out of her sleeping bag. Her feet find the cold ground, and she stands, putting on her boots without bothering to tie the laces. She takes one of the extra flashlights with her, navigating her way through the assortment of tunnels.

Just as she turns the first corner, she hears a faint movement behind her. Aiden is up and following her without a word. She doesn't turn to acknowledge him, knowing that he'll follow anyway. Together, they pace around through the familiar tunnels they've explored throughout the day.

They walk in silence, the only sound the soft shuffle of their footsteps and the occasional drip of water from the ceiling. The beam from Violet's flashlight cuts through the darkness, casting long, moving shadows on the walls. The tunnel stretches ahead, with no destination, no clear path—just the urge to keep moving.

Aiden walks a few steps behind her. He doesn't ask where they're going, doesn't even try to make conversation. Maybe this aimless wandering is what they both need right now. They walk for what feels like hours, the tunnel winding and turning with no real sense of direction.

As Violet angles the light to focus on the wall, it reveals a mural, drawn mostly in what looks like charcoal or graphite. The sight stops them both in their tracks. The mural stretches across the rough stone, a messy tangle of images, each one more unsettling than the last.

There are figures—similar to humans, but twisted and deformed. Some are scrawny, with hollow eyes and elongated limbs, their bodies barely more than shadows. Others are more monstrous, with gaping mouths and claws, their forms surrounded by what looks like tendrils of smoke or fog. Each depiction is different, yet they all share the same underlying menace, the same sense of something wrong, something not meant to exist—because it doesn't.

Violet steps closer, her flashlight revealing more details. The artist, whoever they were, had captured the essence of fear in these images—the kind of fear that settles in the bones and lingers long after the danger has passed. She reaches out, the tip of her fingers brushing the rough lines of one figure, and a powdery layer of black pigment clings to her skin, staining it.

Aiden's voice, low and raspy, breaks the silence. "These look nothing like what I saw."

Violet stays silent as she wipes her stained fingertips on her pants, smudging the fabric as her mind churns. Each swipe leaves faint streaks, but she doesn't notice, too focused on the weight of Aiden's words.

"What did you see?" Violet forces the question out, voice barely a whisper.

Aiden doesn't answer right away. He takes a breath, deep and slow, his gaze still fixed on the twisted shapes before them. When he finally speaks, his voice is low, tight.

"They looked human, at first. At least, their faces did. But their bodies... they were wrong. Twisted, like their bones didn't fit inside their skin. Their limbs were too long, hands like claws, but the worst part was their eyes—or the lack of them."

Violet doesn't move, doesn't speak. She just listens.

"They were sunken, like they'd been hollowed out, but somehow… they moved. They were locked on me, and when they came for me…" Aiden swallows, his voice faltering. His hand clenches into a fist, his knuckles white. "The pain was real. That's what made it worse. Their claws tore at me, and I felt every inch of it. My skin was burning. I…I could feel them dragging me down. I swear I could feel and taste my own blood."

Violet nods, her throat tight. The images are grotesque. *I wonder what Lorenzo saw.*

I wonder…

I wonder what mom and dad saw.

Violet shivers, not just from the cold. The mural, with its disgusting figures and terrifying imagery, seems to pulse with a life of its own, as if the very walls are alive.

They stand there for a long moment, neither willing to look away, neither sure of what to do next.

"What if I'm wrong?" Violet says, the words slipping out of her as she thinks them out loud.

"You're not," Aiden replies without hesitation, his tone steady, reassuring.

But Violet doesn't feel reassured.

"But what if…" She hesitates, her mind racing through every possibility, every scenario where things could go wrong. "What if I'm missing something?"

"I have no injuries," he replies. "No bites, no scratches, nothing. You were right. You *are* right."

They fall silent, the only sound their breath. Violet glances at Aiden, the dim beam of her flashlight catching his face just enough to outline his features. He's standing close, closer than she realized, and she can see the tension in his expression—the tight line of his jaw, the slight furrow in his brow. His eyes are dark and deep, reflecting the faint light.

There's something that makes her heart skip a beat. She's never really noticed it before, how the shadows play across his face, softening the edges. He's handsome in a way that's hard to describe—there's a quiet strength about him, some form of stability that she's come to rely on, even if she would never admit it.

Violet's thoughts start to drift, noticing the curve of his lips, the sharp angle of his cheekbones, and the way his hair falls slightly over his forehead. Her chest tightens, and before she can stop herself, a blush creeps up her neck, spreading across her cheeks. She quickly turns her gaze away, cursing herself for getting distracted with useless feelings. This isn't the time for such thoughts, not here, not now.

She clears her throat, trying to dispel the sudden wave of embarrassment. "We should head back," she says, her voice a little too quick. "We shouldn't be too far away."

Aiden nods, though she catches a slight smile on his lips, as if he's aware of her discomfort and finds it amusing. But he doesn't push, doesn't comment. Instead, he simply turns and starts walking again.

As they walk back to the cavern, Violet can't shake the lingering warmth in her cheeks or the way her heart feels just a little lighter.

Aiden's eyes remain fixed on the ground as he walks. "I wonder if my mom knows something about this," he says slowly, running a hand through his hair. "And if she does know… How come she didn't say anything? She's the reason I'm here."

Violet's pace quickens until she's walking beside him. "Why would your mom know about the fog?" she asks.

"What do you mean?"

"You know what I mean," Violet replies, her eyes narrowing slightly. "Has she been in the Paracosm before?"

His shoulders tense. "Violet. My mother..." Aiden pauses, jaw clenching. "She's—"

"What about your mother?"

Aiden hesitates. "You don't know?"

"Know what?" Violet's brow furrows. "Just tell me."

For a moment, it seems like he might—his lips parting, something heavy weighing on his tongue. But then his eyes flick away. "She's..." Aiden's voice trails off. "You know what? Forget about it."

Violet glares at him. "What? You can't just say that and then—"

"It's nothing," he says, shaking his head with a sigh. "Just forget it."

The silence between them thickens as they continue walking, the atmosphere shifting from strained to something far more uncomfortable. Violet's steps quicken, her flashlight bouncing ahead, revealing nothing but more rock walls and darkened paths. Every so often, she casts a glance at Aiden, who remains a few paces behind, lost in his own thoughts.

After what feels like an eternity of walking in circles, the narrow walls of the tunnel begin to widen slightly. Violet squints ahead, recognizing the faint outline of something familiar. Her heart sinks.

The entrance to the tunnel.

"You've got to be kidding me." She stops abruptly, her flashlight beam flickering across the stone entrance. "We walked the wrong way."

He lets out a small chuckle. "Looks like it."

Violet glares at him, her patience wearing thin. "This isn't funny," she says. "We're supposed to be walking back to the cavern camp, not wandering around like idiots."

Aiden just smirks, unbothered. He steps closer to the tunnel's entrance, reaching out to tap the hollowed-out rock with his knuckles in a slow, deliberate motion.

"Wanna go outside?" he asks.

CHAPTER 10

VIOLET STARES AT him, waiting for the punchline—some sign that Aiden is joking. But then he presses his hand hard against the rock and the tunnel entrance creaks open. A rush of cool night air sweeps inside.

He's serious.

Violet gasps, her breath catching both from the sudden change in temperature and the shock of his audacity.

She watches as the night outside unfolds, the chill in the breeze sending a shiver through her. Her instincts scream at her to refuse. There's nothing out there for them, nothing except the unknown and whatever horrors come with it.

No.

She should turn around, go back to the cavern camp, and never entertain his reckless ideas again. Yet, she doesn't move. Aiden stands there, hand outstretched towards her, a gentle smile on his lips. He's waiting.

"Come on," he says. "We have the masks. We'll be fine."

Say no.

Why is she even considering this? The tip of her fingers twitch in anticipation. Her hand moves without her permission, hesitating in the air, slowly inching towards his.

Turn around.

Leave.

It would be so easy to refuse. It would be safer. But her hand reaches out anyway, her fingers brushing against his. Before she can change her mind, she grips his hand, and he pulls her gently towards the outside.

The air outside feels different—crisper, sharper against her skin. Almost synthetic. The sky above isn't that sick whitish gray anymore. Now it's deeper, almost black, the same color of storm clouds just before they open up. Yet it isn't complete darkness. There's a faint light to it, enough to make out the jagged silhouettes of the crumbling buildings and twisted trees surrounding them.

The wind lingers, lifting grains of sand and dirt into the air and scattering them around their feet in small, swirling wisps of dust.

The world outside is quiet.

Too quiet.

Aiden slides the rock shut behind them with a heavy, muted thud. They stand still, Violet's hand still clasped in Aiden's, his grip firm and somewhat warm.

For a moment, neither of them moves.

"This place could almost trick you into thinking it's peaceful." Aiden's voice breaks the silence. He speaks quietly, but his words drag out, filled with an odd sort of wonder.

Violet doesn't reply. She doesn't need to. Her eyes are fixed on the sky. The absence of the moon leaves a void she hadn't realized she missed so much. No moon, no stars— nothing but that oppressive, dark-gray expanse overhead. She remembers the village, how the stars used to blanket the sky, sharp and clear, without the haze of dust and pollution that shrouded the city.

Here, in the Paracosm, they're gone.

A strange ache settles in her chest, not for the moon, not even for the stars, but for the things she left behind—the small, beautiful things that made the world feel just a little less broken. The loss of her parents. The people from the village. Lorenzo's death. The prototypes left in the cabin.

Violet's fingers tighten around Aiden's, the air sharp against her skin. After everything that happened, tonight feels unnaturally still—until it isn't.

A faint rustle stirs from the darkness ahead.

Footsteps.

Violet freezes, her body locking up with the sound. Aiden reacts faster, stepping in front of her, his body tensing, ready to shield her from whatever hides in the darkness. The air between them vibrates with the restless stir of the wind, and for a moment, all she can hear is the sound of her own breath. Her pulse thrums in her ears. She lets go of his hand, and steps beside him, shoulder to shoulder.

"Who's there?" Violet asks. Her voice is steady, but her heart pounds so hard it feels like it might break her ribs.

There is nothing but silence.

Then, she sees it.

Not the full figure, just a flash—something round and cold, glinting in the dim light. The shape catches the edge of the moonless sky, army green and metallic, a rubbery sheen that is unmistakable.

A gas mask.

The mask's filter gleams just for a split second, and in that instant, Violet's mind snaps back into clarity.

Got you.

Violet's heart thunders as she breaks into a sprint, the ground rushing beneath her feet. This is what she's been looking for, and she can't lose it now.

"Violet, wait!" Aiden's voice calls out, swallowed by the night.

She doesn't slow down. The night blurs around her, a canvas of shifting shadows and indistinct shapes. Every corner, every crevice looks the same, every sound echoing off the nothingness, disorienting.

Then it hits her again—a sudden, damp heaviness in the air. The fog, seeping in, curling around her. Her breath catches, vision narrowing, the world turning into smudged splotches of gray.

Instinct kicks in. She yanks her mask up, fumbling to secure it tight against her face. She glances behind her, catching a brief glimpse of Aiden adjusting his own mask. The fog is coming in faster, stronger than usual, so thick that his face is nothing but a shadowed blur.

She drives herself harder, her legs moving in a frantic rhythm, heart pounding, lungs burning. The fog swallows everything in her vision, but she can't afford to stop.

Not now.

The figure turns a corner, the flicker of its movement barely visible through the darkness. Violet doesn't hesitate. She leaps forward, her boots slipping slightly on the gravel. She falls, pain flaring as her cheek grazes the rough ground.

She stretches out her arm, fingers clawing through the fog, and just as the figure's outline wavers, she grips tight. Her fingers close around a solid ankle, dragging the person down with her.

They collapse with a muffled thud, the weight of the fall sending ripples through the fog. Violet scrambles to her knees, pulling herself up and tightening her hold on the ankle. They try to writhe free, but Violet's grip is firm.

The figure twists around violently, moving so fast that they manage to wrench free from Violet's grip by kicking her back, causing her to lose her balance. With a swift motion, they slam into Violet, pinning her down to the gravel. Violet's arms are forced to the ground, her chest crushed under the weight of her attacker.

A glint of metal catches her eye. The figure's hand moves towards their waistband, and Violet's heart races. The cold, hard barrel of a gun emerges, the weapon unmistakable even in the dim light.

Panic surges through Violet, but before she can react, Aiden's silhouette emerges as a dark shadow against the fog. He wraps his arms around the attacker's torso, locking his grip tightly by their underarms.

The figure struggles, their efforts to reach the weapon growing frantic. Aiden's hold tightens, his muscles straining as he keeps them from drawing the gun. The attacker kicks and writhes, their demeanor violent and desperate.

Violet's breath comes in ragged bursts, her pulse pounding in her ears. She watches, her fear mingling with adrenaline, as Aiden and the figure engage in a fierce struggle. The gun remains out of reach, but the tension in the air is still palpable.

The figure's hands, slick with the grime of their struggle, find their way to Violet's face mask as she attempts to get up. With a sudden, wrenching pull, they yank it away from her face, the fabric tearing free with a sharp sound.

Violet gasps as the cold night air hits her lips and nose. Her breath quickens, each inhalation feeling more exposed, more vulnerable.

"Violet, stay with me!" Aiden's voice cuts through the chaos, strained and urgent. "Hold your breath!"

Violet's chest tightens, her lungs already protesting as she forces herself to hold her breath. Every part of her instinct is screaming at her to inhale, but she resists. Her vision blurs at the edges, spots of black creeping into her sight, her head swimming with the mounting pressure. Each second stretches into an agonizing eternity, her lungs burning, muscles tensing with the effort of keeping still.

Don't breathe.

Don't breathe.
Don't breathe.
Then it becomes unbearable.
Shit.

She gasps, pulling in a desperate breath. The cool night air rushes inside, sharp and biting—and tainted. The fog is quick to seep into her lungs, its bitter taste scraping down her throat like shards of glass. Her nose stings, a burning sensation spreading through her sinuses as if the air itself is tearing through her. Tears well in her eyes, uncontrollable and blurring her vision even further, but not enough to dull the searing pain.

Panic explodes in her chest, her breaths coming ragged and shallow, each inhale only bringing more fog into her body. Her throat constricts, and she coughs violently, her body rejecting the air but needing it all the same. She tries to blink through the tears, her eyes red and raw, but the sting only grows worse.

Aiden says something, but his voice becomes a distant echo in the fog, muffled and barely audible through her choking gasps and the ringing in her ears. The world swims around her, the shadows twisting and warping as her body starts to buckle under the fog's assault.

Violet's world twists and bends around her, the fog curling and pulsating into strange shapes, warping the air into a shimmering, unnatural white landscape. Her vision blurs, turning everything into indistinct shadows. Aiden and the attacker fade into the background, until even their silhouettes dissolve into the fog, swallowed by the sickly shades of white and gray.

This is not real.

She blinks, trying to focus, but the fog feels more and more alive—pressing in, swallowing and devouring everything. Her head throbs, and faint voices seem to whisper from every direction, calling out her name.

"Violet..."

Her heart stutters. The voice isn't Aiden's. It's softer, prettier—yet somehow haunting. The fog shifts, and a black outline appears just beyond her reach, dissolving into the mist before she can make sense of it.

She swallows, her mouth dry, her eyes burning.

None of this is real.

The whispers grow louder, surrounding her.

"Violet..."

Shapes flicker in the corner of her vision—indistinct, shifting figures that seem to grow clearer the longer she stares. At first, they're just blurs, like shadows caught in the corner of her eye. But then they start to take form—a human form, but wrong. Twisted. Their limbs too long, their bodies stretched and contorted as if they've been pulled apart and stitched back together.

This is not real.

Her pulse races. The figures drift closer, moving without sound, their forms flickering in and out of existence. Violet squints, her vision clouded by the fog, trying to make sense of what she's seeing. Her breath comes in short, ragged gasps, and her eyes sting with the tears that blur everything into smudges of gray.

Not real.

Through the haze, she catches a glimpse—a face.

It's gone before she can process it, swallowed by the fog, but her stomach twists. The fog warps again, the voices growing louder, more insistent, more distorted, as the shadows close in.

"Violet... why didn't you help us?"

The voice cuts through her.

She freezes, her legs shaking, every muscle in her body going rigid as the figure in the fog moves closer, materializing from the mist. At first, it's nothing but a mass of shadow, shifting and pulsing, its form warping as if the fog itself is alive. The air thickens, stinking of rot and decay, and Violet can't tear her eyes away.

Two monstrous figures lurch forward, their bodies twisting and bending, sickening cracks of bone echoing through the silence. The one on the left is impossibly thin, its skin hanging and dangling like shredded fabric, revealing darkened veins beneath. Limbs elongate, stretching too far, fingers curling into claws. Its chest heaves, every breath a wheezing rasp as its body contorts. The shape struggles, writhing, its grotesque face rippling with movement.

Not real.

Violet's breath hitches as she feels the second figure closing in. She glances over, just in time to see another nightmarish distortion—an inhuman form folding in on itself, arms twisting at impossible angles, legs buckling and reforming. Its face cracks, bone jutting through in places as the monstrous mass slowly gushes a black goo from all joints.

They're closing in, both monsters cracking and contorting, as if shapeshifting, until—with a snap—they reshape into something she recognizes.

Her father.

Her mother.

Not real.

Not real.

Not real.

The transformation is so abrupt that she stumbles, losing her balance and falling backwards. Her mother's white dress flows, pure and untarnished, looking just as pretty as she remembers—as if she was dressed for a wedding every day.

Her father stands there, unmoving, wearing his police academy uniform, its deep blue fabric torn and smeared with dirt. His once crisp collar is frayed, and the silver badge on his chest is dulled by grime. A thick, graying mustache sits above his tight-lipped mouth, and deep, tired bags under his eyes.

Their pale skin glows against the gray fog, but there's something wrong. The way their necks tilt, just slightly too far, and their eyes... hollow, empty.

And their faces—their faces are not right. Their skin is sagging, dark circles carved into the flesh like someone hollowed them out. Their lips twitch into a grim, twisted smile, and their voice, faint but clear, calls out to her in union. "Why didn't you save us, Violet?"

Violet gasps, her chest tightening. She tries to back away, but her limbs feel heavy, unresponsive.

"I—I didn't know," Violet stammers, her voice trembling. "I didn't know what to do. I was so scared."

Her mother steps forward, her bare feet dragging across the dirt with a sickening scrape. The white dress ripples unnaturally, as though the fabric itself is part of her skin, crawling over her skeletal frame. The edges of her form begin to warp, the pristine fabric of the dress darkening, twisting. Her father follows, his once-rigid posture slouching, his broad shoulders curling inward, bones creaking with each step.

"You left us." Their voices boom louder now, the union of their tone splintering into something unnatural, something that shakes the ground beneath her. Their faces stretch and distort, mouths pulling into grotesque snarls. Their skin peels away in ragged chunks, exposing raw, decayed muscle underneath.

"I didn't mean to!" Violet's hands tremble as she lifts them in front of her, covering her eyes, pleading. Her breath comes in short, frantic bursts, the foul fog burning her throat. The air reeks of rot, sour and bitterness. "I—I couldn't save you! I didn't know how!"

Her mother's hands curl into claws, the skin turning gray, jagged veins bulging beneath. She tilts her head at an impossible angle, her neck cracking as it elongates, mouth stretching wide, lips peeling back to reveal rows of sharp, bloodstained teeth. "You abandoned us!" she screeches, her voice a shriek that seems to tear through her eardrums, rattling in Violet's skull.

Her father is no better—his uniform now hanging in tattered strips, patches of his face shedding off as his mouth warps into a twisted, lop-sided shape. His fingers extend grotesquely, knuckles cracking as they grow into razor-sharp talons, reaching for her.

"Violet!"

Violet tries to scream, but the air is gone. She can't breathe. The fog has thickened, coiling around her, slipping inside her throat, choking her. The world blurs into a black void as her parents continue to twist, their forms growing larger, towering over her. Their voices become a cacophony of rage, hissing and rising in intensity until it feels like they are screaming inside her brain.

"Violet!"

Cold, slimy tendrils slither up her legs, pulling her down, trapping her. She's sinking, drowning in the very earth beneath her. The air stinks of iron and decay, filling her nose until her eyes burn with tears.

"I'm sorry," she sobs, her voice a hoarse whisper, barely audible over the grotesque sounds surrounding her. "I didn't know. I couldn't... I'm so sorry..."

"Violet, wake up!"

The world around Violet shifts, the monstrous forms of her parents flickering and fading. Her vision swims, her breath coming in jagged gasps as the fog swirls and dissipates. She rubs her eyes hard, palms pressing into them until her eyelids sting. Each time she pulls her hands away, the surrounding night feels more solid, more real.

She rubs her eyes again, and the grotesque figures melt into a puddle of darkness. The smell of rot and decay lingers in her nose, but it's faint now, fading with the last remnants of the hallucination. The air clears. She can breathe again.

Her heart pounds in her chest, the sound almost deafening in her ears. The ground beneath her is solid, no longer dragging her down into the earth. She takes a shaky breath, her hands trembling as she wipes at her eyes one more time. The fog is gone.

Aiden's voice breaks through the ringing in her ears. "Violet... it's over."

Aiden is kneeling beside her. He's right there, solid, tangible—real. He's pinning down her attacker, their body slack and unmoving beneath him, gas mask still on. The attacker's face is hidden, but it doesn't matter anymore. They're real. This is real.

Aiden reaches for her, his fingers brushing against her cheek, wiping away a stray tear. His touch is gentle, grounding, and the last of the nightmare finally begins to dissolve. He's holding her hand now, and the warmth of it pulls her fully back to reality.

The hallucinations may have been caused by the fog, but the emotions are real. The guilt, the fear, the memories. It all presses down on her, making her feel so small, so fragile.

Violet throws herself into Aiden's arms, wrapping her arms around his neck, burying her face against his shoulder. His jacket is rough against her skin, his scent earthy, and she clings to him like he's the only thing keeping her from falling apart completely.

Her sobs come in waves, uncontrollable, each one wracking her body as she holds onto him. Aiden holds her tight, his arms encircling her, his hand stroking her hair gently, proving to her that this—this moment—is real.

"You're ok. Everything is ok," Aiden says.

I'm ok.

Everything is ok.

CHAPTER 11

VIOLET STEPS INTO the tunnel, her limbs heavy and mind still reeling from what just happened. The cool air inside rushes over her, but it does little to calm the heat spreading across her skin. Her eyes adjust to the dim light, catching the sight of Elliot leaning against a stone wall.

Elliot's face lights up as soon as he sees her, whistling sharply with two fingers. A moment later, Ellie appears from the shadows, her footsteps fast and frantic.

Ellie rushes forward, arms outstretched. "We've been looking everywhere for you!" she exclaims as she throws her arms around Violet's shoulders. "You just disappeared—we were so concerned!"

"I'm sorry," Violet says.

Ellie's hand moves up, brushing against Violet's cheek. Her fingers pause as they graze over the scratches and dried blood marking her skin. "Your face..." Violet doesn't respond, and Ellie's hand shifts to rest on her forehead. "You're burning up," Ellie mutters, her eyebrows furrowing together.

The heavy sound of footsteps echoes behind them. Aiden emerges from the darkness, his face grim as he steps into the tunnel, not bothering to close the rock entrance behind him. Draped over his back is the limp, unconscious body of the person in the gas mask. The extra weight makes his movements slower, but he manages to carry them effortlessly inside.

Ellie's eyes widen as she spots the figure slumped against Aiden. "There was a person in a gas mask after all," she says, her voice low. She takes a cautious step forward, eyeing the mask. "I wonder why they wear this... You think they know about the fog?"

Aiden lays the figure down on the stone floor, rolling his shoulders as if shaking off the weight.

Violet crouches beside the unconscious figure, her eyes scanning the still form. She watches the slow rise and fall of their chest, confirming they're still breathing—still alive. "It looks like a woman," Violet mutters, glancing back at Aiden.

Aiden straightens, his hand slipping into his pocket as he pulls out a small, white device. "Whoever she is," he says, "she definitely knows something." He holds up the object between his fingers—a small box, barely the size of a matchbox, with a single miniature lever, similar to a light switch. "We had a bit of a fight. She was desperate to protect this thing."

Ellie steps closer, scanning the object. "What is it?" she asks, her gaze flickering between the device and the unconscious woman.

Aiden shakes his head. "No clue. But when I flipped the switch... the fog disappeared."

Ellie's eyes widen in shock. She glances over at Elliot, who's been quietly following the conversation, his eyes narrowing as he reads Aiden's lips. Ellie swallows hard, her voice faltering for a second. "So... someone's controlling the fog?"

Elliot crosses his arms, his expression one of disbelief, but there's an edge to it—fear, perhaps, or something stronger, closer to anger.

"Not only is the fog poisonous... someone's behind it. It's insane," Violet says.

A tense silence falls over the group, the faint hum of distant wind echoing through the tunnel. Violet's gaze flickers to the unconscious figure, the gas mask still obscuring her face. "We should take it off," she says quietly, more to herself than anyone else.

Ellie bites her lip. "But what if... I mean, what if it's booby-trapped? We don't know this person or where she comes from."

Aiden sighs, running a hand through his hair. "We can't keep her like this forever. If she's dangerous, we need to know why. And if she knows anything about the fog or who's behind it... we need answers. Now."

Violet looks at Aiden, then at the others. She hesitates for a moment, but then she nods. "He's right. We can't stay in the dark any longer."

Ellie shifts uncomfortably, glancing at the gas mask. "But what if removing it makes things worse?"

Violet kneels down beside the masked woman, her hand hovering just above the hem of the mask. "We don't have another choice." Her voice is calm, but her heart hammers in her chest.

Aiden crouches beside Violet, the unconscious body between them. His hands tremble as he gently moves Violet's hands away. He hovers over the gas mask, fingers just above the straps. The tunnel is silent, each of them holding their breath. Even the wind outside seems to still and watch. His fingers graze the cold, rubber surface, hesitating for a heartbeat. He looks up at the others. Violet's jaw is clenched.

Ellie is standing rooted in place, wide-eyed while biting her nails. Elliot's hands curl into tight fists at his sides.

"Here goes nothing," Aiden mutters under his breath.

He unclips the mask, the snap of the release echoing inside the tunnel. He slowly lifts it away. The mask comes off in slow motion, revealing the face beneath.

And they all freeze.

Gemma.

Aiden flinches backwards, throwing the mask to his side. Violet gasps, the sound sharp and raw. Her heart stutters in her chest, a sickening swirl twisting in her stomach. Ellie's hand flies to her mouth. Even Elliot, normally composed, falters, his breath hitching as his gaze locks onto the familiar face.

Gemma's face is dirt-smeared, her eyes closed, the faint rise and fall of her chest the only indication that she's still alive. But there's no mistaking it.

It's her.

Ellie takes a step forward, her voice trembling. "How... how could she—"

"No..." Violet whispers, stumbling back, her mind racing. "It can't be..." Her words die in her throat, unable to reconcile the woman they knew as nurturing and kind with all the nightmares they've faced in the Paracosm.

Aiden's face tightens, his gaze fixed on Gemma's unconscious body. "This... changes everything," he says, hand resting on his chin. "But it adds up, somehow. She works in the High Council labs. She knows her way around plants... and poisons."

Violet feels her chest tighten, the shock and disbelief intertwining into a single, overwhelming force. Every memory she has of Gemma flashes before her—the smiles, the conversations, the trust. "Do you think Yuka knows? Could she be part of this too? They seemed awfully close," Violet says, her voice shaking.

Aiden's brow furrows, confusion flickering across his features. "Gemma and Yuka? Close?" he says, glancing back at Gemma. "Are you sure? Gemma couldn't stand Yuka during training week."

"I'm sure," Violet insists, her mind replaying the moments back in the forest. "When we found the cabin in the woods, Gemma always seemed overprotective of Yuka. She made sure she kept her out of danger. Every time."

"Hmm..." Aiden's frown deepens. "That's odd."

"How could she do this to us?" Ellie whispers, her voice barely audible.

They stand around Gemma, the weight of the revelation suffocating them. Violet's heart pounds in her ears, the disbelief still sharp and fresh. Ellie's hand trembles at her side, her mind clearly racing with unspoken questions. Aiden's gaze remains fixed on Gemma, his jaw tight with tension, while Elliot watches the scene unfold, eyes narrowed.

Then, a soft groan escapes from Gemma's lips.

Violet's breath catches in her throat. Her body tenses as Gemma's eyelids flutter, her body shifting slightly on the ground. Her fingers twitch first, then her head tilts to the side, a weak gasp for air as consciousness starts to return.

"She's waking up," Ellie whispers.

Aiden takes a step forward, his arm stretching outwards, instinctively moving in front of the group. "Stay back," he warns, hissing through his teeth. "We don't know what she'll do."

Gemma's eyes blink open, glazed and unfocused at first. She coughs weakly, her hand reaching up as if trying to grasp at something invisible. Then her gaze sharpens, confusion flickering across her face as she slowly becomes aware of her surroundings.

Violet takes a step back, the shock of seeing her companion—no, her enemy—awake making her stomach twist.

Gemma's gaze finally lands on them. Her jaw clenches, going stiff, and for a moment, she looks like a cornered animal, fear flashing in her eyes. Then something darker crosses her expression—recognition, guilt, and defiance all at once. Her lips part open, but no words come out.

"What the hell is going on, Gemma?" Aiden growls, his voice sharp as a blade, impatient. His fists tighten, every muscle in his body coiled, knuckles turning white.

Gemma's eyes dart wildly around the room, locking with each person surrounding her. Her breathing quickens, panic setting in as her gaze drops to her waistband. She reaches down, her fingers frantically feeling for the gun she had tried to use on Violet.

But it's gone.

Left behind in the ruins.

Her eyes widen, her movements becoming more desperate. She pats her pockets, searching with a frantic urgency.

Aiden steps forward, slowly raising the small white remote into view, the faint switch gleaming under the dim light of the lanterns. "Looking for something?" he says.

Gemma's face contorts into a mixture of rage and defeat. Her eyes narrow at Aiden, her lips pulling back in a snarl as she tries to push herself up from the ground, muttering a stream of inaudible curses under her breath. But before she can rise, Ellie and Elliot are on her, grabbing her arms and forcing her back down.

Ellie's grip tightens on Gemma's left arm, her jaw clenched, while Elliot locks down her right. Gemma struggles, thrashing against them, but it's no use. She's pinned.

"Get off me! Ginger freaks." she hisses, her voice sharp, venom dripping from every word. Her eyes flicker towards the remote in Aiden's hand again, and for a moment, some form of darkness seems to settle into her gaze.

Violet's fingers curl around the handle of the knife strapped to her leg, the cold steel sliding free with a quiet hiss.

Aiden's voice breaks the tension with a hushed warning. "Violet…" He calls out her name, concern lingering in the air, thick and heavy.

Violet offers Aiden a subtle nod, a silent promise, asking him to trust her. She steps forward and lowers herself to one knee in front of Gemma. She swallows the lump in her throat, her voice low, barely above a whisper. "I can't believe I trusted you, Gemma."

Gemma doesn't respond. Instead, she spits—right into Violet's face.

Violet's eyes flicker with disgust, but she doesn't flinch. She wipes the spit away with the back of her hand, slowly. Her hand moves without hesitation, pressing the edge of the knife to Gemma's throat. The cold metal against her skin makes Gemma stop thrashing, her wild movements halting in an instant.

The room stills as Aiden and Ellie seem to gasp in union, the air growing thick as Violet leans in. "Explain yourself."

Gemma's eyes widen, the fire in them dying for just a moment, the sharp edge of the blade enough to hold her in place, breath shallow and uneven.

Aiden inches closer, his voice gentle but urgent. "Violet, stop."

But Violet can't hear him. All she sees is Lorenzo—his broken body, his lifeless being staring back at her from the dirt. Her chest tightens, rage flooding her senses, overwhelming everything else. The knife trembles in her grip, not from fear but from the raw force of emotion surging through her.

"Did you know?" Violet's voice cracks as she yells, her grip on the knife tightening, knuckles turning white. "Did you know Lorenzo was going to die when we agreed on letting someone stand guard?" Gemma flinches, but it only fuels Violet's anger. Her vision blurs, the memories from the cabin crashing into her thoughts. Her voice rises, breaking with grief and fury. "What happened to the others? Tell me what you did!"

Violet presses the blade harder, and without realizing, she draws blood. A thin crimson line appears on Gemma's throat, the cut shallow but real.

Aiden's eyes widen. "Violet! Stop!" He lunges forward, grabbing her arms. The knife slips from her fingers, clattering to the floor as he pulls her back. Violet struggles against him, her body trembling, her breaths ragged and uneven. "That's enough, little mouse." Aiden's voice cuts through her haze as he holds her back, arms wrapped around her tightly. She fights him, but he doesn't let go, his voice is soft, pleading. "I'll handle it. Please, calm down."

Her vision swims, anger and sorrow blurring together, until finally, her body goes slack in his arms. The weight of what just happened crashes into her all at once, and she gasps for air, her head spinning.

Ellie's voice trembles, her grip firm as she clings to Gemma's arm. "We thought you were our friend," she whispers, the pain of betrayal laced in every word.

Aiden, still holding Violet close, rubs slow, soothing circles on her back, calming her trembling body. With a soft touch, he picks up the knife from the floor, the blade cold and slick from the blood that now stains it. "We'll for sure be reporting you to the Council, Gemma," he says.

Gemma smirks, a twisted, chilling grin stretching across her face. Her lips curl slowly, the smile unnatural, malicious. Her eyes glint with something sinister, a dark amusement flickering within them.

"You mean the people who hired me for quality control?" Her voice is low, mocking, each word sharper than the blade that had been at her throat. "Yes. Go on ahead. I'm sure they'll be thrilled to know I've been doing a good job."

Aiden freezes. The knife slips from his fingers, clattering loudly against the stone floor, the sound echoing through the entire tunnel. His face goes pale as he stares at her, disbelief washing over him.

"You're lying," he breathes out. "My mother would have told me."

Gemma's smirk deepens, the corners of her mouth stretching impossibly wide, a grotesque parody of joy. Her eyes narrow, glinting with satisfaction, a predator reveling in its prey's shock. "Are you sure about that?" she whispers, her words crawling beneath their skin like poison.

Aiden's face pales further, the shock and anger warring for dominance. His eyes narrow as he processes Gemma's smirk and her taunting words. Before he can react further, Violet frees herself from his arms, stepping forward, her voice a low, inches away from Gemma's face.

"What happened back at the cabin?" She forces the words through clenched teeth. "Where are the others?"

Gemma's nonchalant demeanor doesn't falter. She shrugs, a mocking grin curling her lips. "Liam's dead," she says casually, as if discussing the weather. "Yuka ran off with my backpack. The brat left me with nothing. Don't know where she is. Hopefully dead too."

Ellie's eyes widen. "We need to find her. She could be in danger."

Gemma rolls her eyes so far back they look like they could get stuck at the back of her head, her tone dripping with disdain. "Bring her body back if you find her. I'm definitely not getting paid enough to carry all these corpses around. Lorenzo was the worst. That idiot was in bits and pieces everywhere. What a mess. It was disgusting."

Violet's blood boils at Gemma's casual cruelty. Without warning, her hand flies across Gemma's face. The sharp slap echoes through the tunnel, Gemma's head snapping to the side.

Violet's chest heaves with fury, tears of rage and despair blurring her vision. The sting in her hand from the slap is sharp and immediate, her fingertips tingling with a raw, aching need for more. Gemma's head turns back slowly, her expression shifting to a mix of surprise and twisted satisfaction, her gaze cold and unfeeling.

Violet leans closer, her voice a harsh, demanding whisper. "Tell me. Is there a way out of here, you bitch?"

Aiden steps next to her, slightly pulling her back, creating some distance between Violet and Gemma. "While Conrad and I were exploring, we found a tall wall surrounding the Paracosm. We thought it might be our way out. We should go back to our old shelter, get Conrad, and then try to find a way through it."

Gemma's laugh cuts through the tense silence, a chilling, high-pitched cackle that echoes off the walls. It's a sound of madness, a manic glee that seems to seep from her very soul. "Good luck getting out," she jeers, her eyes gleaming with a cold, unhinged delight. "There's no way out without the Council opening the gates."

"Maybe we can jump over the wall," Ellie suggests. "Or build a bridge over it somehow."

Gemma's laugh fades into a cruel, knowing smile. "Oh, but there's no wall," she says. "The Paracosm isn't surrounded by a wall. It's a dome. The sky is fake. The air is fake. Everything is fabricated."

"Stop lying, Gemma," Aiden says. "There is *no* way the Council would be ok with this."

"Not only are they ok with it, but they're also the ones who created this entire thing," Gemma says, her voice growing colder with each word. "The Paracosm is nothing more than testing grounds. And you," she says, her eyes locking onto Violet's with a chilling intensity, "and the rest of the prototypes—are nothing but lab *rats*."

CHAPTER 12

THE SKY SHIFTS into a dull, dark gray with faint traces of lighter shades seeping in. The lighter it gets, the more the transition to morning appears mechanical, devoid of the vibrancy sunrise should bring. A cold wind whips through the ruins, but even that seems wrong—repetitive.

Gemma's hands are bound tight to a weathered pole, her arms pulled back, ropes biting deep into her skin, leaving angry red marks and raw scratches. Her glare cuts through the group, cold and silent, lips pressed into a thin line of defiance. The air around them feels unnaturally sharp. Without the constant threat of the suffocating fog, the world feels exposed, its unsettling silence magnifying every small sound.

Violet's fingers twitch as she glances back at the sky. The cloudless gray seems endless. Her throat is raspy and dry, the tension wrapping around her chest, but there's a strange clarity now. For the first time in what feels like forever, they don't need to hide anymore.

Ellie stands a few feet away, arms crossed tightly over her chest. She watches Gemma without saying a word, her lips puckered into a slight pout. Elliot lingers at her side, his eyes flicking back and forth between Gemma and his sister.

Gemma's voice cracks through the stillness, desperate and strained. "You can't just leave me here. I can help you. Please! Please—just untie me, and I'll tell you how to get out of this place." Her words hang in the air like a lifeline she's clinging to, her eyes darting between all of them, pleading. "We…We can work together."

Violet steps forward, her boots crunching over the gravel, her steps slow. She crouches, meeting Gemma's gaze head on with cold, unwavering eyes. The weight of everything—every betrayal, every lie—presses on her shoulders.

"It's okay, Gemma," Violet says, her voice eerily calm. She tilts her head, her eyes narrowing as a bitter, small smile tugs at her lips. "Your dear High Council will be coming for you eventually…" A flicker of hope flashes through Gemma, but it's short-lived. "…Or for your corpse." Violet's tone shifts, hard as stone, before she turns away.

Gemma's breath catches, her face twisting with panic as she pulls against the ropes. "Wait—Violet! Everyone! Please!" The group follows Violet as she walks away, not bothering to look back. Gemma thrashes and screams, begging, but her pleas are swallowed by the emptiness around them.

Aiden walks beside Violet, their fingers brushing together every now and then as they lead the group deeper into the ruins. The wind weaves through the crumbling structures, carrying with it the same stale scent of dust and decay that seems to cling to every corner of the Paracosm.

Soon, they come upon Aiden and Conrad's old shelter—a makeshift construction built into the edge of the ruins.

However, something captures their attention even more than the shelter.

There it is.

The wall.

A tall and dark metal structure, towering above them — an impenetrable barrier. Its surface is smooth and cold, reflecting the faint light of the fake sky. The wall stretches upward, much taller than the wall surrounding the wealthy part of the city. It's far too high for any of them to scale or jump over without serious equipment.

Violet steps forward, her breath catching in her throat as she sizes it up. It's not just tall — it's a trap, a cage, built to hold them in.

To hold all the prototypes in.

Every single year.

She bends down, picking up a jagged small rock from the ground, her fingers gripping it tightly. With a sharp intake of breath, she hurls it towards the sky above the wall. For a moment, it arcs through the air, but then —

BZZZZTT!

The rock seems to hit something invisible. The sky above the wall flickers. It's an electronic panel. It's fake, just as Gemma said it would be. The seamless and monotonous gray glitches just for a split second with a dull electrical hum, sparks crackling in the air.

The others stare, wide-eyed. Violet's fingers twitch at her side, her pulse quickening. After so many schemes and lies, Gemma was telling the truth. They were trapped in a dome, with no escape unless the High Council wished it.

The ruins appear less worn-out around them as they move further into the wreckage. The air feels heavier here. These houses — what was left of them — stood taller than the others. Dilapidated, yes, but still standing, with crumbling walls and roofs that sagged but hadn't yet collapsed.

Aiden slows his pace, his gaze scanning the area. He motions for the others to stay quiet.

Then, they hear it—faint, muffled commotion coming from inside the nearest building. The sound of something moving, or someone. A low thud. A scraping noise. Violet's heart skips a beat.

"Conrad?" Aiden's voice is barely a whisper, his brow furrowed. Without waiting for a response, he moves towards the shelter.

The door to the building is warped and broken, hanging off its hinges. It's wedged shut, seemingly sealed from disuse, but the sounds inside grow louder—like something or someone is struggling.

Aiden takes a deep breath, the muscles in his jaw flexing. Without hesitation, he slams his shoulder into the door, the wood splintering with a dull crack. The door gives way, flying open with a shower of dust and debris. The air inside is stale, suffocating. Violet coughs as the dust rises around them, her hand instinctively covering her mouth.

Inside the shelter, a surprising scene unfolds.

Yuka, her small figure darting around the room, is hanging garlands of paper stars from the crumbling beams. She hums quietly, seemingly oblivious to their arrival or the tension in the air. The paper stars sway, their edges slightly frayed.

Conrad, sitting on a large rock in the center of the room, has his index fingers pressed against his temples, rubbing small circles. He looks worn out—exasperation carved into the lines of his face.

Conrad lifts his head, and the moment he sees Aiden, relief floods his expression, though it's tinged with a trace of annoyance. He stands up slowly, stretching his back like he's been sitting there for far too long.

"Finally," he sighs. "Someone normal with some common sense. Please," he gestures towards Yuka, "take this child away. I've been babysitting her for like two days, but it feels more like two decades. I can't take it anymore. I'm going insane." Conrad tugs at his own hair, right eye slightly twitching.

Yuka twirls in the background, her paper stars casting faint shadows against the walls. She flings a paper necklace with surprising accuracy, and it lands right on Conrad's head, settling like a crooked flower crown. He freezes for a second, blinking as Yuka grins mischievously.

"Don't be silly, Connie. We're the same age," she teases, her eyes sparkling. "We should be friends."

Conrad's face flushes as he rips the paper necklace off, tearing it into pieces in one swift motion. "For the millionth time... My name is Conrad!" His voice is sharp, filled with the exasperation of someone who's been dealing with this for far too long. He turns to Aiden, his gaze flickering with confusion when he spots Violet. "Wait, what is she doing here?"

"She's with me," Aiden replies, his voice calm but firm, as if that's all the explanation needed.

Yuka's eyes widen as she finally notices Violet and the twins standing in the doorway. "Violet! Ellie! My favorite girls!" she exclaims, abandoning her paper stars and running toward them, arms open wide.

Ellie barely has time to react before Yuka throws herself into a hug, squeezing them both tightly while giggling.

Conrad, meanwhile, rolls his eyes dramatically and flops back onto his rock, rubbing his temples once again as if this entire situation is giving him a headache. "I swear..." he mutters under his breath. "I'm so done with this kid."

Ellie smiles, pulling back from Yuka's embrace. "It's nice to see you're doing good, Yuka," she breathes out, her tone gentle and sincere.

Yuka pouts, crossing her arms with a dramatic sigh. "You guys, Gemma is a meanie," she declares with a mixture of annoyance and indignation. "We're not friends anymore."

Conrad rises from his rock and ambles over to the group, his demeanor shifting from irritation to something more serious. "Oh, right. Yuka found Gemma's backpack," he says, reaching into the bag and pulling out a couple of worn notebooks. "It's packed with all kinds of freaky lab stuff. Turns out the fog—"

"We know," Aiden interrupts, cutting him off before he can finish.

"No, listen," Conrad insists, flipping through the pages of one of the notebooks. "The Paracosm is the Council's way of making sure the people of St. Marrow aren't growing immune to the fog. We're literally lab—"

"Lab rats?" Violet interjects, a smirk creeping onto her lips as she finishes his sentence. Her expression is a mix of satisfaction and bitterness, bringing them back to their first encounter in the Paracosm.

Conrad opens his mouth to respond, but Aiden beats him to it. "We found Gemma running around in a gas mask. She had a remote that controls the fog."

"We left her tied to a pole," Violet says as her face darkens. "She also says there is no way out."

"Dude, you think your mom knows about this?" Conrad asks, his voice edged with disbelief. "She forged the picks to have you sent here. That's seriously messed up."

"I don't know," Aiden replies, his gaze drifting to the ground between them. "I've been wondering the same thing."

"Aiden, why would she be involved? What's going on with your mother?" Violet asks, slipping her arm around Aiden's lower arm, pleading for answers.

Conrad's gaze sharpens. "Excuse me! Who even are you to be touching him like that?" he gasps, his hand covering his mouth. "How dare you? Aiden is—"

"Conrad, don't," Aiden interrupts, or at least tries to.

But Conrad presses on, ignoring Aiden's attempt to stop him. "You know who he is, right? Son of the great Sophia Cardinal—yeah, the new ministress. He's trained his whole life to follow in her footsteps someday. People like him—well, people like us—don't mingle with..." Conrad pauses and looks Violet up and down. "...with the rats."

Violet releases Aiden's arm, her expression hardening as she turns in slow motion and meets his gaze. "Your mother..." she says, drawing out the words, "is a High Council member?"

"Yes. She's the new head of the Ministry of Conspiracy and Espionage." Aiden's face reddens. "I know you must have questions, but I can explain."

"Explain what?" Violet's voice rises, her eyes flashing with anger. "That you were hiding that from me?"

"I wasn't hiding anything, I swear!" Aiden's voice cracks. "I was shocked too when I realized you didn't know. Everyone does. The only people who don't are—"

"Let me guess," Violet interrupts, her tone sharp. "The rats?"

"The people from the village, Violet!" Aiden's frustration boils over. "The villagers usually don't attend the ceremonies."

"Oh, maybe because we're not welcome in the city!"

"How is that my fault?"

"I never said it's your fault!" Violet shouts. "But your mother is just like—"

"Just like what?" Aiden fires back, his eyes narrowing.

"Just like the rest of them!" Violet's voice shakes with fury. "He just said it—she went out of her way to send you here, knowing you could die. The High Council doesn't give a single *fuck* about who lives or dies in St. Marrow."

"I've got questions too, but I can promise you my mom's not like that."

"Don't fight, you guys." Yuka pops up between Aiden and Violet, her eyes sparkling with excitement as she interrupts their argument. "I can't wait to make friends with all the others!"

Aiden and Violet stare at her, their quarrel momentarily forgotten. "What others?" Ellie asks.

Yuka beams. "Well, if the fog is fake, that means we don't have to stay in St. Marrow anymore, right? We can get out. We can meet all the people in the entire world and the universe," She says, twirling around.

A stunned silence follows. Violet's breath catches as the thought takes hold. St. Marrow has been her entire world, a city surrounded by an impenetrable wall of fog for as long as she can remember. The idea of stepping outside—of leaving behind everything she's ever known—feels both exhilarating and terrifying.

"But… there is nothing out there, right?" Ellie's voice is soft, uncertain, as if she's trying to reassure herself. "St. Marrow's supposed to be the last civilization alive. Has been for over a century."

Conrad rolls his eyes. "They lied about the fog," he says with a shrug. "I wouldn't be surprised if they were lying about that too."

The thought consumes Violet, the thought of a life beyond the fog—a world they've only heard rumors and stories about. Could there really be more beyond St. Marrow?

Her mind drifts away, painting vivid scenes of a world she's only ever imagined. She envisions rolling fields of green grass, lush and vibrant, in stark contrast to the dying, brittle patches around the city. She pictures a sky awash in hues of blue—brighter and more alive than the endless gray that stretches above St. Marrow. The same blue sky she's glimpsed in old pictures and vintage books.

"We need a plan," Aiden's voice cuts through her daydreaming, grounding her back in the present. "We need to get out of here."

"But how?" Conrad asks.

"We need to figure out how to get past that wall," Aiden continues, his gaze steady as he looks around the room. "And we need to be prepared for whatever might come next."

Violet nods, brushing away the remaining traces of her daydream. The image of a better world still lingers at the edges of her thoughts, mixing with the unanswered questions still hanging in the air from her argument with Aiden.

Yuka paces excitedly, her hands flailing as she speaks. "We could dig underneath the wall! It's not that deep, right?"

Conrad snorts, shaking his head. "You've seen how thick the ground is. Even if you could dig through it, the earth's packed tight. Plus, there's probably more steel underneath, reinforcing the dome."

"Violet found a tunnel," Aiden says. "But there was no mining equipment inside."

Ellie's eyebrows furrow together. "What about trying to scale the wall? We could use some of the debris from around here."

Violet shakes her head, her gaze drifting to the wall. "Even if we could find something sturdy enough, the wall's too high. It's sheer metal. We'd never make it up, not without proper climbing gear."

Elliot nods, index finger resting on his chin.

"Even if we did somehow manage to climb it, what's to stop us from getting shocked by the electric panels?" Aiden says. "Gemma said they're wired to prevent escape."

The group falls silent for a moment, considering all their options—or lack of options. Violet's fingers tap repeatedly against her thigh. "What if we try to find a way to shut down the electric panel?"

"That's a dumb idea," Conrad scoffs. "We don't know the wiring or how to disable it without getting electrocuted ourselves. And there's no guarantee the panel isn't booby-trapped."

Yuka's enthusiasm seems to fade from her face as she listens. "Maybe... maybe we can find something in the ruins, something we missed before?"

Aiden glances around, his gaze scanning the remains. "We've scoured this place already. Every corner, every nook. There's nothing we haven't seen."

They throw around a few more solutions, and all of them have been weighed and found lacking, leaving them with a sobering conclusion: leaving the Paracosm will require more than just a clever idea—it will demand patience, and perhaps a bit of luck. The group falls into silence, each of them lost in their own thoughts.

"I know how to cheer us up," Yuka says as her gaze lingers on the electric panels of the fake sky, her eyes sparkling. "Sparkles!" She reaches into her necklace and pulls out a firecracker, its bright red wrapping a stark contrast to her pale small hands. With a quick flick of her wrist, she tosses it at the spot where Violet had previously thrown the rock.

The firecracker arcs through the air before landing on the metal surface with a soft clink. It erupts in a burst of noise and light, the panel flickering erratically. Sparks fly from the spot where it hit, and the screen that once displayed a gray, artificial sky now flashes wildly. The panel's display shifts from normal to a chaotic red, an error message blaring across it in glaring, angry letters.

Violet's eyes widen. "Keep going, Yuka!" she urges, her voice edged with desperation. "Do that again."

Conrad, standing nearby, rolls his eyes and lets out a harsh laugh. "That's foolish. You're both insane," he says, shaking his head. "You don't know what you're doing. You'll just make things worse."

Ellie's brow furrows as she watches the chaos unfold. "I actually agree with Conrad this time. We have no idea what will happen if we set off alarms or get the High Council's attention. It could be dangerous."

"That's exactly the point," Violet says. "If they're alerted, they'll have to come and check it out."

Aiden's eyes widen as he completes her thoughts. "And if they come to investigate, it might give us the opportunity we need to find a way out or at least gather more information."

The corners of Violet's lips twitch into a small smile. His support bringing some warmth to the cold tension swirling between them since the argument.

Yuka's fingers dance along the beads of her necklace, her expression a playful mix of mischief and pride. "Should I use my beads?" she says, her eyes twinkling. "They're made out of explosives."

Ellie's head snaps towards her. "No explosives!" she says, voice cracking slightly. "That's too dangerous."

Yuka's giggle rings out in response as she ignores Ellie's concerns with a light, dismissive wave of her hand. "Okay, okay," she says, grinning as she plucks another firecracker from her necklace instead. She flicks it between her fingers, ready to throw.

Yuka's movements become rapid, almost frantic, as she hurls one after another at the flickering panel. Each firecracker explodes in a burst of sound and light, creating a cacophony of noise that echoes through the ruins. The panel's display goes from erratic flashes to a full-blown chaos, each burst of light turning a deeper, more ominous shade of red.

Sparks shoot from multiple metal panels, sizzling against the backdrop of the now crimson sky. The once muted gray light of dawn is drowned out by the violent flashes of the firecrackers. The sky starts to ripple, its surface now turning into a frenzied, pulsating sea of red and black.

SYSTEM FAILURE

ALERT: MALFUNCTION

WARNING: SECURITY BREACH

The error messages covering the panels flash and overlap, creating a disorienting whirlwind of text.

A shrill, mechanical wail pierces the air—a siren, loud and unrelenting, ripping through the silence as if the

Paracosm itself is screaming. It builds in intensity, a maddening spiral of noise that echoes off the crumbling walls, vibrating through their bones.

"This is too much!" Ellie says as she clutches her ears, her face contorted in a mix of terror and frustration. "We need to stop this!" she shouts over the blaring alarms, but her voice is barely heard.

Conrad, his eyes open wide with horror, scrambles to hide behind a crumbling wall, his skepticism replaced by genuine fear. "This is madness!"

Yuka throws the last firecracker in her hand, her eyes wild and unfocused, as the alarm's shriek crescendos. The dome is now a swirling vortex of flashing lights, red blares, and erratic text, the very air around them vibrating with the intensity of the sound.

Aiden grabs Yuka by the shoulders, shaking her. "Yuka, stop! This is going too far!"

A low, grinding sound echoes from above, causing them all to look up. The line where the towering metal wall meets the glitching red panels begins to shift, stretching apart with an eerie groan of metal on metal. The separation reveals a hidden row of vents lining the perimeter of the Paracosm.

The vents hiss open with a sharp, mechanical whine, and in an instant, thick, undulating fog spills out in a relentless flood. It pours into the air, sweeping across their vision like an opaque tidal wave. The world around them warps and fades, visibility shrinking to mere inches as the choking mist engulfs them.

"Everyone!" Violet screams as she covers her mouth and nose. "Wear your masks!"

Aiden, Ellie and Elliot all scramble to put on their face masks, their movements frantic and desperate. Violet's hands fumble as she tightens her straps, her breaths coming in short, sharp bursts.

Aiden rushes over to Conrad's side. "Conrad, cover your face!" he shouts, his voice muffled. Conrad, wide-eyed and disoriented, fumbles for a moment before Aiden grabs his shoulder, pulling him closer. "Use your turtleneck—now!" Aiden commands, and Conrad hurriedly yanks the hem of his navy sweater up until it covers half of his face.

Violet's eyes flick to Yuka, who stands mesmerized by the swirling fog. "Yuka, cover your face!" she screams, but Yuka remains motionless, entranced.

Her eyes are wide, fixated on the tall metal wall. She doesn't make an effort to cover her face—instead, she gazes at the fog with a dreamy, almost childlike wonder. Her fingers dance in the air as if reaching out to touch the intangible, her face glowing with an eerie fascination.

"It's so… so pretty," Yuka murmurs, dragging out her words. "Like fairies and shooting stars. Can I play with you guys? Can you teach me how to fly too?"

Without a trace of fear, Yuka walks away from the group, her movements eerily serene. Her necklace, now tattered and frayed, hangs loosely around her neck, its strings and beads giving way under the strain of the firecracker explosions.

Violet takes a step towards Yuka, her voice shaky as she calls out, "Yuka, come back!" But before she can get any closer, Aiden's hand clamps around her arm, pulling her back tight against his chest.

Yuka's necklace snaps, beads scattering and rolling across the sand around her feet. The instant they touch the ground, there's a deafening, blinding flash—a violent eruption that rips through the air.

Yuka's body disintegrates in a horrific display. Flesh and blood burst outwards in a shower of gore. The blast sends chunks of her torn skin and muscle spraying through the fog, mingling with the dense, choking mist. Her limbs are torn apart, scattering in grotesque, disjointed pieces across the ground. Blood splatters and sprays with a sickening splat, coating the area in a grim, crimson sheen.

The remnants of her body are spread about like a macabre jigsaw puzzle. Violet's cheek is sprayed with a warm, sticky splash of blood, a vivid streak of red staining her skin.

CHAPTER 13

THE SMELL OF burnt flesh clings to the air, bitter and pungent, mixing with the metallic scent of blood and the fog. Ellie's wail shatters the silence, the sound so visceral it seems to crawl under everyone's skin. She clings to her brother like she's about to collapse, her sobs muffled by the mask but unrelenting, shaking her frail frame. Elliot holds her tight, his face hidden in the hollow of her shoulder, his own breaths ragged.

Violet stands frozen, her eyes wide and locked on the red splatter that stains the cracked sandstone, on Yuka's remains scattered around. At first, it's as if her brain can't process it. Yuka, the girl who had just been laughing and twirling, now a jagged mess of blood and bone. Violet's face mask presses against her skin, her breath quickening, coming in short gasps, burning her lungs. The fabric rubs against her mouth, wet with tears she didn't realize were falling down her face. Each sob that escapes her feels like it's clawing up her throat, desperate for release.

Aiden's hand touches her shoulder, light at first, as if he's unsure if he should even try to comfort her. His fingers tremble, and when she looks up at him, his eyes are wide, the outline of his jaw clenched tightly beneath his mask.

Violet's grief feels trapped inside her, building pressure until she thinks she might burst, just like Yuka had. The thought makes her stomach churn, and she squeezes her eyes shut, trying to block it all out—the blood, the panic, the sharp tang of death that lingers in the fog. But it's everywhere, sinking deep into her bones.

Aiden tightens his grip on her shoulder, pulling her closer as if that will somehow make it better, but nothing feels real anymore. The fog presses in on all sides, thick and suffocating, and the memory of Yuka's cheerful voice echoes in her mind, only to be shattered by a repetition of the deafening crack of the explosion that had ended her.

Conrad's voice cuts through the suffocating silence, harsh and loud. "The wall!" he shouts, pointing towards a rough opening where Yuka's explosive firecracker necklace had blasted a hole. His hand trembles, and for a moment, no one moves.

A way out.

Then, almost as one, they run.

Violet's legs feel heavy, the ground beneath her unstable as her boots kick up dust and debris. The echo of Ellie's sobs follows right behind them, but the thudding of their feet drowns it out. Violet tries to focus on the breach in the wall, the only possible way out of this nightmare, out of the Paracosm, but her eyes betray her. Against her will, her gaze darts to the place where Yuka had been just moments before.

And she regrets it instantly.

Bits of charred flesh and bone are scattered like debris among the remains, tangled with the snapped fragments of Yuka's necklace. Dark red sludge drips from shards of stone, pooling in small puddles where limbs should be. Her stomach clenches as her eyes, despite her attempts to look away, catch sight of chunks of muscle, twisted and gnarled, stuck to the dirt.

Aiden reaches out, grabbing her arm as they approach the hole. "Don't look," he whispers, though his voice is tight, like he's barely holding it together himself. But it's too late. Violet's already seen too much. The taste of bile rises in her throat, and she can feel her pulse hammering in her ears, drowning out the world as they scramble through the gap.

They run without looking back, their breaths ragged, feet pounding against the uneven ground. The piercing blare of the Paracosm's alarm screams behind them. They push forward, legs burning, lungs screaming for air. The noise follows them like a ghost, relentless, but the farther they go, the more it fades—until it becomes nothing but a distant hum, swallowed by the eerie silence of the outside world.

Violet's legs finally give out beneath her, and she collapses to her knees, a cloud of dust and sand swirling up around her. Her body trembles, chest heaving in a desperate attempt to catch her breath. The face mask is suffocating her, constricting around her face, hot and claustrophobic.

She claws at the straps, tearing it off with frantic hands, gasping as the cool air hits her face. But the relief is short-lived. The air is thick and heavy, and no matter how hard she inhales, it feels like there isn't enough oxygen. She coughs, collapsing further onto the dirt, hands splayed out as her head swims with dizziness.

Aiden kneels beside her, his own breath uneven, his face pale and sweat-slicked under the mask. "Violet..." His voice is rough, almost broken.

Ellie stumbles, her eyes wide and unfocused. Her hands shake uncontrollably as she presses them to her temples, a frantic murmur escaping her lips. "We can't... we can't just leave her there," she says, her voice trembling. "We have to go back. We can't just—"

Ellie breaks off, her words dissolving into sobs as she clutches her head tighter, tugging at her own hair. Her breaths come in sharp, shallow gasps, her chest rising and falling with panic.

Conrad stops near the twins. "We can't go back," he says.

"We can't leave her like that…" Ellie says again, but her voice is quieter now, almost a whisper. She takes a stumbling step toward the direction they came from, but Elliot grabs her arm gently, pulling her back.

He signs something, his hands slow and his expression pained, his own eyes glistening with unshed tears. There's a gravity in his hands as they move, the message clear even without words. Ellie watches him, her breath hitching in her throat, her sobs intensifying.

Before she can speak again, Elliot pulls her into a tight embrace, cradling her head against his shoulder as she cries into his chest. Her sobs are muffled but raw, each one a broken sound that pierces the cold, empty air.

None of them ask what Elliot signed.

None of them have the courage to.

A low, rhythmic hum fills the air, a sound so subtle at first that it almost blends into the distant alarm still echoing faintly behind them. But the longer they're away from the Paracosm, the louder the noise seems to grow — mechanical, guttural, like metal grinding against metal, pulsing in slow, ominous beats. The ground beneath their feet seems to vibrate with each echo.

"What's that sound?" Aiden asks, tension creeping into his words.

"I hear it too," Violet replies, her eyes narrowing as she gets back on her feet.

Conrad freezes mid-step, his face paling as he lifts a trembling hand, pointing into the distance. "Look," he whispers, his voice barely audible over the eerie buzzing that now surrounds them.

Violet's heart stutters as she follows his gaze, her eyes widening in horror.

In the distance, looming like monstrous sentinels, stand massive vents. The structures are huge—towering, skeletal frames of blackened metal, their surfaces slick with condensation. The metal seems to pulse with life, faint creaks and groans echoing from within the hollow depths of the machines. Thick, mechanical tubes snake out from the base of each vent, twisting and curling like the gnarled roots of some ancient, long-dead tree.

From the mouths of these machines, flowing trails of fog are spat into the air, dark and churning, as though the gears are breathing out the very nightmares of the Paracosm. The mist is dark gray, almost black, swirling and coiling like smoke, heavy and dense. It rolls over the ground in great waves, swallowing the horizon and devouring the landscape.

Each hiss of the vents is deafening in its unnaturalness, a sickening metallic sound that cuts through the thick air, scraping against their ears like nails on rusted iron. The fog spills out fast, forming a massive, turbulent cloud that stretches toward the sky, blotting out what little light remained, leaving everything in an oppressive darkness.

Violet's breath catches in her throat, her entire body tense, a sickening sense of dread curling in her stomach. The vents pump out the fog with increasing intensity, and the cloud spreads, blotting out the skyline, swallowing the world whole.

Her legs tremble as she turns in a slow circle, taking in her surroundings. Her boots kick up small clouds of dust as she steps, the barren landscape crunching beneath her feet. The land is lifeless—just miles of cracked earth and jagged rocks. There's no sign of vegetation, no remnants of civilization beyond the ruins they've just fled. Everything feels off, wrong in a way she can't quite put her finger on.

After a full turn, she traces the fog's edges, unsure of what she's actually looking at. The shadowy shapes appear to be nothing but more debris and old abandoned buildings, barely visible through the heavy mist.

She squints, her heart pounding harder, leaning forward as the shapes loom larger. The fog shifts, and for a moment, her breath catches.

It's not just rubble.

It's too structured, too precise.

Something tugs at her memory, but it's only when she spots a high point piercing through the haze that the realization slams into her like a punch.

Violet's stomach drops. She knows that silhouette.

The unmistakable shape of the clock tower.

St. Marrow.

Her heart hammers against her ribs, the realization crashing down on her like ice water.

"That's..." Violet hesitates, the words catching in her throat. What if it's just another illusion? Her mind, twisted by fear, playing tricks on her. No... it couldn't be. She squints, her pulse racing. She knows that tower—the one that looms over the city, dictating their lives, their curfews. She'd recognize it anywhere. Violet exhales sharply, almost in disbelief. "That's St. Marrow," she whispers, her voice trembling.

"We're outside the city?" Conrad mutters, squinting into the distance. He raises a hand above his eyes, as if it could somehow help his gaze pierce through the thick fog. "Oh! I see the clock tower."

Elliot signs something, and Ellie, still trembling and streaked with tears, nods. "You're right…" Ellie says. "That means there's actually nothing outside the city."

"This is great news!" Conrad claps twice. "We know the fog is harmless if we don't breathe it in. That means we can at least go back to the city. It's better than staying out here."

"No," Aiden says, his voice is firm. He steps forward, his eyes darting back and forward between the vents and the cloud of fog. "We can't go back. They'll figure out we escaped from the Paracosm. They'll know what we've seen. What we know. They'll be coming for us."

"Do you have a better idea?" Conrad scoffs. "Do you want to stay here and wait for death? To die out here instead of inside the Paracosm. Is that really any better?"

"First, we need to find shelter," Violet says as she scans the bleak wasteland for any potential hiding spots. "Anywhere we can hide from the High Council."

Conrad opens his mouth to argue, but his words are cut short by the distant rumble of machines. The sound grows louder, a deep, menacing growl that seems to vibrate through the ground beneath their feet.

Their heads snap towards the sound in unison, eyes narrowing against the haze. In the distance, blurry dark shapes begin to emerge, barely visible.

Monsters?

An illusion?

Violet's heart skips a beat as the shapes sharpen—black vans, sleek and threatening, cutting through the fog with their engines roaring.

Aiden takes a step forward, eyes locked on the vehicles. "They must be responding to the alarm," he says. "Going to see what's wrong with the Paracosm."

For a brief moment, a flicker of relief crosses Violet's face. But it vanishes just as quickly, her stomach twisting in dread. She shakes her head, urgency rising in her voice. "We need to move—and fast. Once they see the hole in the wall, they'll know some of us escaped."

Ellie's breath catches as she glances back at the ruins. "And when they find Gemma… she'll tell them everything," she says.

But then, without warning, the vans veer off course.

The tires screech, kicking up a cloud of dust and sand as they swerve sharply, aiming directly for the group. Through the fading fog, the High Council insignia on the side of each van gleams like a death sentence.

"Run! They're coming for us!" Violet's voice cracks, panic twisting inside her throat.

In an instant, their feet are moving—desperation propelling them forward. There's no plan, no escape route. Just the raw primal urge to escape.

They run, though there's nowhere to go.

The wasteland stretches ahead of them, miserable and empty. No trees, no rocks, no shelter. Just an endless expanse of desolation beneath a dead gray sky. The ground crunches beneath their feet—dry, brittle, lifeless. Their frantic footsteps echo across the barren landscape, but the roar of engines grows louder behind them, vibrating through the earth like the approach of an unstoppable predator.

Every breath Violet takes feels razor-sharp, cold cutting through her lungs as she pushes her legs to move faster.

The vans are closer now.

Violet knows deep down they can't outrun a van—it's impossible. But still, her legs keep moving, driven by an instinct she can't control. The thought flickers in her mind, a cold truth she tries to bury beneath the pounding of her heart. It doesn't matter. She runs anyway, because stopping feels like surrender, and surrendering means death.

They keep running.

They keep running towards nowhere.

The emptiness presses in, suffocating. The eerie, silent wasteland offers no cover, no salvation—just an endless horizon of nothingness. The air is thick with dust and powdered gravel. They're exposed, utterly helpless.

Aiden glances over his shoulder, his face pale with terror. "They're getting closer!" he shouts, though they all know it. The sound of the vans fills their ears, drowning out everything else.

The world around them is dead. Their shadows stretch out before them, elongated and distorted by the city headlights that slice through the fog.

Ellie stumbles, catching herself before she falls, her breath coming out in ragged sobs. "We can't—" she gasps, but her words are lost in the void. "I can't take it anymore!"

"Keep moving, Ellie! Don't stop!" Aiden yells, his voice ragged and breathless, each word strained.

Violet's chest tightens. Her legs scream for rest, her lungs burn, but she knows if she stops, they're done for. The black vans loom behind them, devouring the distance like a nightmare made real.

The High Council is closing in.

It's only a matter of time before they catch up with them.

They'll kill us.

All of us.

CHAPTER 14

THE BLACK VANS all screech to a halt, forming an ominous ring around the group. The sharp squeal of the brakes pierces the air as the doors slam open with a loud bang, one after the other. Violet's heart pounds like a war drum in her chest, the air catching in her throat as dark figures spill out from the vehicles, faces obscured by sleek black helmets. Weapons are immediately leveled at them, cold metal barrels gleaming in the gray light.

Violet freezes, her pulse surging in her ears.

This is it.

I'm going to die.

Panic grips her, raw and suffocating. They've been caught. No trial, no mercy—just a swift execution to ensure the High Council's secrets die with them. Her mind races through every grim possibility, each one ending with them lying lifeless in the dirt, their bodies discarded as collateral in a dirty conspiracy too vast to fight.

The oppressive silence that follows is shattered as Sophia—head of the Ministry of Conspiracy and Espionage, Aiden's mother—pulls down her own black mask. Her sharp features are hard, eyes cold but focused, her presence commanding the attention of every terrified soul standing frozen in place.

"Mom?" Aiden's voice cracks as he stares at the woman he clearly hadn't expected to see, especially not here. His shock is a palpable weight in the air.

Sophia's eyes flicker briefly towards Aiden before landing on the others, her operatives standing still behind her. She makes a sharp gesture with her right hand, and without a word, the soldiers lower their weapons but remain watchful. "Get inside the van. Now," Sophia orders, her voice clipped, leaving no room for argument.

Violet's body freezes in place as she hesitates. She casts a glance at Aiden, her mind racing with all the reasons not to trust anyone from the High Council. Aiden meets her gaze, his expression hard, giving her a sharp nod before stepping inside the van without a word. Reluctantly, she follows, the weight of dread heavy with each step as she climbs in last, the van's dark interior swallowing her whole.

One of Sophia's subordinates slams the van's door shut behind them, and with a low rumble, the engine roars to life as they speed away.

The inside of the van is nothing like what Violet expected—cold, sterile, lined with sleek silver panels and harsh overhead lights that cast long shadows across their faces. The walls are smooth, reflecting the faint outlines of equipment—monitors displaying strange, fluctuating graphs of vitals, red dots pulsing in tandem with heartbeats. There are restraints hanging from the ceiling, their dangling chains rattling with every bump in the road, and everything smells faintly of disinfectant and metal, the scent sharp and acrid in her nostrils. The seats, hard and unforgiving, line the walls in a militaristic grid.

Violet's eyes dart around the confined space, landing on the walls plastered with surveillance monitors, each one flickering with live feeds—mostly static, but some showing bursts of the outside world, grainy images of the Paracosm's fog, the outskirts of St. Marrow, and the city itself.

"Strap in. We're not safe yet," Sophia commands.

Violet's gaze flicks towards the voice, her breath catching in her throat as she sees Sophia up close for the first time. Sophia stands with an air of control, her sharp features framed by raven-black hair tied back in a severe bun. Her skin is flawless, lightly bronzed, with a touch of ageless elegance. There's an effortless grace about her, a calculated precision in her movements—an older, more dangerous version of Aiden. The resemblance is striking: the sharp cheekbones, the piercing gaze that holds a depth of intelligence. But where Aiden's eyes are clouded with kindness, Sophia's are sharp as razors, cold and unreadable. Her red lips curl into a faint smile as she glances back at the group.

Sophia's fingers glide over a sleek control panel, her voice calm but commanding as she gives rapid orders to her subordinates. "Double back to the east. Ensure no pursuit from the Council's forces. And keep the scanners active for any—"

"Did you purposely send me to my death?" Aiden's voice cuts through the air, sharp and accusing, echoing in the confined space of the van.

The tension crackles. For a moment, Sophia's hands freeze mid-motion, her cool demeanor faltering. Slowly, she turns to face him. The silence stretches, thick and heavy. Then, with an exhale, she speaks—her tone calculated but not devoid of something resembling regret.

"I've been tracking your vitals the entire time," she admits. "You have a chip, implanted years ago. It monitors your heart rate, oxygen levels—everything. I knew exactly what you were going through inside the Paracosm. The moment something went wrong, I was ready to pull you out."

Her words hang in the air, but they clearly don't offer the reassurance Aiden hoped for. His eyes flash with disbelief, anger simmering beneath the surface. "That doesn't answer my question. I wasn't selected as a prototype during the picks. *You* added me to the list. If you knew about the fog…then why?"

Sophia's gaze narrows slightly, her lips tightening. "Lucius had eyes everywhere. I couldn't risk showing my hand too soon. If I acted before I had proof of his agenda, everything we've worked for would be in jeopardy."

There's more to her words—more she's not saying. Violet can feel it too, watching the two with a growing unease, wondering if Sophia's protective instinct truly runs as deep as she claims, or if Aiden is merely a pawn in a larger game.

"Who cares about Lucius? What does he have to do with this?" Aiden's jaw tightens as he leans forward, his frustration palpable. "You could have warned me. You let me walk into hell without telling me a damn thing. Why? Why, mom?"

Sophia's eyes meet his, and her voice lowers, sharp and cold. "Because I didn't have a choice."

Aiden's brow furrows, confusion flickering across his features. "What?"

Sophia inhales deeply. "Lucius threatened me." Her words come out fast, almost mechanical, but there's a flicker of bitterness behind them. "He discovered things—things from my past. Obscure methods I used to rise through the ranks of the High Council, until I became one of them."

Violet watches Aiden's face shift from confusion to realization, the tension in the van tightening like a trap. "He… He knows?"

"He agreed to keep quiet about it—under one condition."

Aiden's face pales. "You're saying—"

Sophia nods, her lips curling into a grim line. "He wanted you, Aiden. You as a prototype. If I didn't comply, he would've exposed everything I'd done, destroyed everything I've built. Sending you into the Paracosm was the only way to buy time."

Aiden recoils as if struck. "You used me as a bargaining chip."

Sophia's eyes harden, but there's a trace of guilt buried beneath her mask of control. "I had no choice, Aiden. I couldn't just sit back while Lucius twisted the Council to his will. I needed time to gather information—time to uncover what was really happening inside the Paracosm. And... I thought, with me tracking your vitals, I could keep you safe."

Aiden slams his fist against the side of the van, the sound echoing in the tense silence. "You didn't keep me safe, Mom! You threw me into a death trap without even warning me! Some of my friends died in there!"

Sophia's eyes narrow, her jaw clenched tight as she leans against the cold steel wall of the van. "I did my best, Aiden. You weren't there to make friends. We came for you as soon as we could."

"You did your best?" Aiden's laugh is hollow, bitter. "Did you also do your best when you let dad die?"

The words hang in the air like a sharp blade, slicing through the fragile connection between them. Sophia's shoulders tense, and for the first time, her confidence falters. She turns away from him, her back straightening as if absorbing the blow, but she says nothing.

Violet watches the exchange in silence, her chest tightening. Aiden's words pierce the air, raw and unfiltered. The tension in the van is suffocating, a thick, invisible pressure that seems as asphyxiating as the fog.

Sophia stands rigid, staring at the cold metal floor beneath her feet. The silence that follows is more damning than any defense she could muster. She doesn't deny it. Doesn't argue. Instead, she lets the silence speak for her.

Her back remains to them, as though turning away can shield her from the truth—or from the eyes of her son.

One of Sophia's assistants, a young man with sharp features and an air of cold efficiency, steps forward, holding a sleek hand scanner similar to the one the guards had used on Violet when they first captured her at the police academy. His movements are precise, detached, as he moves through the group, the scanner emitting faint beeps with each pass. Aiden's face scan flashes green, then Ellie's, and Elliot's—all of them cleared without much reaction.

When he reaches Violet, his gaze sharpens. He pauses, eyes narrowing as he lifts the scanner, the device humming ominously as it passes over her. There's a slight glitch, a flicker of confusion on his face. He turns his attention fully to her. "Who are you? Why don't you have a face ID?" he asks, looking down at his clipboard. "And why were you in the Paracosm? Your name isn't on the official list of prototypes."

The air in the van thickens with tension as all eyes fall on Violet. Conrad narrows his gaze, his tone dripping with judgment. "You seriously don't have a face ID?"

She takes a deep breath, trying to appear calm despite the tightening knot in her stomach. "I was pronounced dead when my parents disappeared in the fog five years ago and… I was sent to the academy on a rescue mission," she begins, her voice steady but laced with the exhaustion of everything they'd just been through. "Dr. Parcel… he hired me to stop him—" she points toward Conrad— "from entering."

"Dr. Parcel?" The assistant repeats.

Violet pushes through, words tumbling out now. "I don't even know what's real anymore. He said his parents wanted him safe but… I'm not sure what Parcel's true motives were, or if anything he said was true."

For a moment, there's silence. The assistant's eyes flicker towards Sophia, seeking direction. And then, a subtle reaction. Sophia, standing at the front of the van, frowns deeply at the mention of Dr. Parcel's name. Her lips press together in a thin, hard line, the unease unmistakable.

"Can we… can we just go back to the city?" Conrad asks, his voice low and wary.

Sophia turns back towards the group, her expression unreadable. "Back to the city?" she echoes. Her gaze shifts to each of them, lingering longer on Aiden before settling back on Conrad. "It's not that simple."

"Why not?" Ellie asks.

Sophia moves to a console, tapping something on a touchscreen display, and an array of encrypted files flashes across the screen. "Lucius," she says, her voice tight with restrained anger, "has been making his moves for years. Slowly, quietly, consolidating power in ways most wouldn't notice until it's too late." Sophia's fingers move swiftly across the display, pulling up documents, images, footage—all tied to Lucius. "I've uncovered evidence that he eliminated multiple new ministers. A lot of staged accidents and disappearances. But that's just the start. Lucius has a larger plan—one that goes far beyond simple control and the Paracosm." She pauses, her eyes flicking to Aiden. "His end goal is nothing less than total power. He wants to become the sole ruler of St. Marrow."

Ellie sucks in a sharp breath, her face going pale. The weight of Sophia's words settles over them. This wasn't just about the Paracosm experiment anymore—this was about the entire city. Their home. The fragile structure they'd always believed would keep them safe was crumbling, and now they were tangled in the web of the High Council's lethal political games.

Violet's stomach twists, the dread that had been gnawing at the edges of her mind now fully consuming her. "So… what does that mean for us?" she asks, her voice barely above a whisper. "What happens now?"

Sophia's face hardens. "Now? Now, you're all liabilities. He knows you've escaped. You know too much. You've seen too much. Lucius won't rest until every loose end is tied up."

The group falls into a tense, uneasy silence.

They had escaped the Paracosm, but they were far from safe.

"What about the people from the village?" Violet asks, her voice trembles as she speaks. Her eyes search Sophia's face for any sign of empathy. "You can't just leave them. They're starving—dying." She clenches her fists, thinking back to the desperation in the villager's eyes, the hollowed faces of those she left behind.

Ethan.

Ingrid.

The children.

"Lucius will only act in favor of those who bring him profit and power. The village… it's nothing to him. Less than nothing." She leans back, arms folded, her voice hard as steel. "He won't spare a thought for them."

Violet feels her chest tighten. Every moment in the Paracosm—the monsters, the fear, the deaths—it had all been for the chance to help her people, to bring back hope. "No," she says, her voice firm. "We need to get to the village. They can't be left to die."

Sophia meets Violet's defiant stare, her brow furrowing slightly as if weighing something. She sighs, conceding. "We will get there. But only when I can guarantee our safety. Going now would be suicide. You can't help them if you're dead."

Violet's mind spirals, her thoughts a tangled mess of doubt and fear. Sophia is part of the High Council—she's one of them. The very people responsible for the Paracosm, for the horrors they'd barely escaped. How could she trust someone so deeply entrenched in the system that had nearly killed them? But Sophia is Aiden's mother. And she had come to save them. Violet's chest tightens.

For now, she would have to trust her.

"Excuse me, ministress Sophia." Ellie's voice breaks the tense silence, a tremor of fear threading through her words. "My brother, Elliot… he's still sick. The fog made him sick.

He needs medical attention." Her eyes glisten with unshed tears, the weight of her words pulling at the frayed edges of her fake composure.

Sophia nods slowly. "I can help," she says, her voice steady. "I have access to medical supplies and personnel who can treat him."

The van jerks to a sudden stop, the tires crunching against gravel and loose dirt. The low rumble of the engine fades into silence, and for a moment, no one moves. Violet feels her heart lurch as the van sways slightly, the only sound the faint creak of the van settling into place. Then, the door slides open with a sharp hiss, letting in a gust of cold air that stings her skin.

Sophia leads them out of the van. Around them, the landscape stretches out in jagged formations—crooked trees and rocks twisted by time and neglect, casting eerie shadows in the fading light. The horizon is empty, the sky hanging like a gray sheet above them, oppressive and still.

"Here," Sophia says, striding toward a pile of uneven rocks that look no different from the others. She runs her hand along the rough stone until there's a faint click, almost too quiet to notice. A door creaks open from within the rock itself. Dust spills out as the metal door shifts, revealing a dark stairway that spirals down into the earth.

The door closes behind them with a heavy thud, sealing the outside world away.

Inside, the air shifts—cooler, clinical, buzzing with the hum of unseen machines. The walls are made of sleek steel, polished and cold to the touch. As they descend, the corridor opens up into a sprawling chamber, lit by a sterile, bluish glow that casts long shadows across the floor.

"Welcome to the Oasis," says the same assistant who had scanned their faces earlier, offering a brief smile in Violet's direction.

The Oasis.

The Oasis feels more like a military base than a refuge. Walls lined with consoles flicker with data feeds, maps, and holographic projections. Security footage from above plays on some screens, tracking movement in the wasteland, while others display schematics of the Paracosm and St. Marrow. Along the far wall, rows of weapons gleam under the harsh lights.

To the right, the medical station sits stark and sterile with reflecting harsh overhead lights. Shelves lined with neatly organized medical supplies stand ready to address any injuries and illnesses. Across from it, there's an armory filled with an assortment of weapons and gear meticulously arranged.

In the center, a meal distribution area buzzes with subdued activity. Tables are set up, where a few weary individuals sit, scooping food onto their plates from large metal containers. The aroma of a simple stew wafts through the air, mingling with the scent of disinfectant. As people eat, quiet conversations fill the space, their voices a mix of fatigue and relief.

Sophia moves them ahead past all of it, always issuing orders to some of her subordinates, while others remain stiff and wary. Though they're hidden from the High Council for now, the cold steel walls of the Oasis offer little to no comfort.

It's a place built for survival, not peace.

CHAPTER 15

SOPHIA TURNS TO her subordinates, giving brisk orders. "Bring each of them to an empty capsule," she commands.

Violet blinks rapidly.

Capsule?

She exchanges a brief look with Aiden, her mind racing with questions, but there's no time to ask as one of Sophia's assistants gestures for him to follow.

Before Violet can make sense of her thoughts, a young man approaches her. He exudes confidence and charm, his movements smooth as he steps in front of her. He stands tall, not quite as tall as Aiden, but still towering over Violet, with black hair that falls just above his sharp jawline. An easygoing smile tugs at the corner of his lips.

"You can call me Riku," he introduces himself, voice steady, almost teasing. "Guess I'm your guide now." His eyes twinkle with a mix of smugness and friendliness, and he gives a small bow, exaggerated enough to make it clear he doesn't take himself too seriously. "So, ready for the grand tour of your capsule?"

Violet stares at him, caught off guard by the shift in energy. His composure is palpable, and she isn't sure whether to be annoyed or amused by his attitude. "I don't really have a choice, do I?" she mutters.

"Nope," Riku replies, flashing a grin. "But don't worry, I'll make sure you feel right at home." He winks, then motions for her to follow him. "This way."

Home.

As they walk, Riku casually glances back at her, either sizing her up or making sure she's still behind him. "You look like you've been through hell and back," he comments, his tone light. "But hey, you survived the Paracosm, your face can't be scanned. Not everyone can say that."

Violet remains quiet, her mind racing.

What's his deal?

Riku leads Violet through a sleek, well-lit corridor, the hum of machinery pulsing all around them. The air feels too clean, like something out of a laboratory, every corner meticulously controlled. Violet's boots echo against the metal floor, the sound swallowed by the faint beeps and clicks of the surrounding technology. She can't shake the feeling that this place is alive in some way, breathing through the wires embedded in the walls.

"Isn't it amazing? The Oasis," Riku says, breaking the silence. "It's meant to be a safe haven. Off the radar. The High Council can't touch this place, or at least, they haven't figured out how to yet." His tone carries an edge of smug pride, like he enjoys the fact that he is part of something this secretive.

Violet's eyes dart to the cold metallic walls and the subtle blue light that stretches along the ceiling. "And what exactly do you do here?"

"Oh, a bit of everything." He smirks. "We're not just hiding out. We've got supplies, weapons, tech. This place is more than just a bunker—it's a fortress, a sanctuary." He glances at her, eyes gleaming. "Don't look so tense. You'll be safe here."

She doesn't respond, her stomach knotting tighter as they continue down the corridor.

They stop at a door marked by a glowing panel that softly hums in the sterile air. Riku fishes out a small, slim card from his pocket and hands it to her. "Here. This is your key card. Wear it around your neck. It's your way in and out." He leans in closer, so close she feels his breath against her skin as he whispers, "Also avoids questions. A single swipe of this thing will grant you access to pretty much anything around here."

Violet takes the card, its cold surface pressing against her palm. As she slips it over her head, Riku manually taps a code into the panel, and the door slides open with a quiet hiss.

"Your quarters," he says with a slight bow, the smirk never leaving his lips. "After you."

Violet steps inside, her breath catching at the sight of the room. It is small, round, and stark white, like a sterile pod. The walls are smooth, unbroken except for soft ambient lights embedded in the ceiling that wash the room in a calming, dull glow. It feels alien, too clean. A small, circular window is cut into the far side of the wall, but when she peers through, all she can see is white.

The furniture is sparse—a round, oversized bed takes up most of the space, its pristine white sheets contrasting sharply with Violet's grimy skin, dirt and sweat clinging to her. A tiny desk tucks into the corner, barely making the room feel lived-in. The faint scent of antiseptic lingers in the air, sharp and pungent.

"Comfy, right?" Riku leans in the doorway, his smirk softening for a brief moment. "You'll get used to it."

Violet doesn't respond, simply nodding, her mind still swirling.

It's so…

Impersonal.

Empty.

Riku steps closer, his fingers grazing the key card before letting it dangle around Violet's neck. "Don't lose that. It's your lifeline here," he says, his voice smooth. "And if you ever need help... well, you know who to ask." His teeth are a blinding shade of white, and his eyes linger on hers a little longer than necessary. He turns to leave but stops when the door beeps and Aiden bursts inside.

Aiden's gaze flicks between Violet and Riku, narrowing ever so slightly as they lock onto Riku's lingering hand near her. With a huff, Aiden strides over, intentionally bumping shoulders with Riku as he passes.

Riku doesn't budge. "I'll be taking my leave, m'lady," Riku says, his tone dripping with mock formality, making Aiden's jaw tighten. He shoots her a wink before the door slides shut.

Violet watches Aiden for a moment as he lets himself flop down into her bed, noting the stiffness in his shoulders as he stares up at the ceiling. She shifts on her feet as she takes a seat at the edge of the bed, taking little to no space.

"How did it go with your mom?" Violet asks.

Aiden doesn't answer immediately. Instead, he reaches over and takes her hand, intertwining their fingers with a surprising gentleness, the warmth of his touch standing in contrast to the cold sterility of the room. His thumb grazes her knuckles, and for a brief second, it's like they're somewhere else—anywhere but here.

He sighs, finally looking at her. "You ask too many questions," he teases, though his smile doesn't quite reach his eyes. "But hey—looks like we're capsule neighbors now." His voice carries a forced lightness, trying to brush off the weight of everything. Aiden lifts his free hand, gesturing vaguely toward the walls, trying to coax a laugh from her. "Bet my capsule's got a better view, though. Your white is not quite as white as mine."

Violet smiles faintly, the corners of her lips lifting. His attempt at humor works, if only a little, breaking through the tension. But she doesn't miss the way his grip tightens ever so slightly around her fingers, as if grounding himself.

"Capsule neighbors, huh?" she echoes.

"If you hear snoring, don't blame me. That's Conrad right across from us. He sounds like a tractor when he sleeps." Aiden gives her hand a small, tender kiss, his lips brushing her skin softly.

Violet lets out a soft laugh, the sound surprising her—it feels like ages since she's allowed herself to laugh like this. But the warmth of the moment fades almost as quickly as it comes. Her smile falters, the heaviness settling in her chest again. "Aiden…" Her voice grows quieter, more serious, and she gently pulls her hand free from his.

"Wait—did I… was that too much?" He blurts out, panic lacing his voice. "I—I didn't mean to make things weird." He stumbles over his words, his gaze searching hers. His fingers twitch, and he shifts slightly.

Violet blinks, startled by his reaction. "No, Aiden, it's not that…" She shakes her head.

"I need to get to the village," she says, her voice firm now. "I can't just stay here while the people who looked after me my whole life are starving and dying—or worse. I promised them I'd come back."

Aiden sits up straighter, clearing his throat. "Violet, it's not safe," he says. "My mom told me the High Council's already looking for us. They're probably scanning every corner of the city. If we go back now, we'll be walking straight into their hands."

"I don't care." Her voice trembles slightly, not from fear, but from the weight of the responsibility she's taken on. "I can't just hide here. If I don't do something now, more people will die. I never meant to enter the Paracosm—it was my chance to help them, to make it all worth something. I wanted to give back to them."

Aiden stares at her for a moment, his jaw tight.

With a heavy sigh, he stands up, moving closer to stand in front of her. "If you're going, then I'm going with you," he declares, his voice steady. There's no hesitation, no doubt. "There's no way I'm letting a small mouse like you go out there alone."

Their eyes meet, and for a moment, the room feels smaller, the walls closing in on them. In the stillness of the capsule, a heavy silence settles between them, punctuated only by the soft hum of the facility outside.

Violet's heart races, not just from the urgency of their situation but from the warmth radiating between them. Aiden's hand lingers near hers, his gaze softening as it drifts to her lips. For a brief second, the world outside seems to disappear, and nothing exists but the air between them.

Aiden leans in, his breath brushing against her skin, and her eyes flutter shut, the tingles of anticipation dancing on her lips.

A sudden knock shatters the moment before it even happens. The door swings open, and Ellie steps inside, her eyes widening in surprise at the sight of Aiden and their proximity.

"You guys have to see this," she breathes out, slightly out of breath, her voice laced with urgency.

Violet and Aiden exchange a quick glance, curiosity pulling them to their feet. They follow Ellie out of the capsule and into a spacious meeting room that buzzes with an electric energy. The walls mirror the ones inside the van, lined with screens displaying real-time data, the air thick with the scent of coffee and anxiety.

At the center of the room stands a large screen, its surface flickering with a live feed. As Ellie guides them inside, Conrad, Elliot, and Sophia are already there, standing in tense silence. Their eyes are glued to the screen, faces reflecting the dim glow of the broadcast.

On the screen, the image sharpens to reveal Lucius, his face a mask of calculated control, addressing the citizens of St. Marrow.

"Salutations, my dear citizens of St. Marrow," Lucius begins. His polished tone carries across the room, echoing off the walls. "I regret to inform you that the Paracosm experiment has concluded, and, tragically, no one has survived this year."

Violet feels a chill crawl down her spine. Her gaze darts to Aiden, whose face is locked in disbelief.

"They were all prototypes," Lucius continues, his tone growing darker, almost mocking. "Sacrificed for the greater good. This experiment, as always, comes at a price. A necessary one. Let this serve as a reminder to all of us: the risks we face, the dangers that lurk just beyond our walls, are very real." He pauses, his eyes scanning the crowd on the screen with a cold, calculated gaze. "But it's not just the fog we must fear. Those living beyond the city walls have proven time and time again to be weak, vulnerable, unable to contribute to the strength of St. Marrow. Their survival can no longer be guaranteed."

Those living beyond city walls?

Does he mean the people from the village?

Violet's stomach tightens as Lucius' words pierce through her. She clenches her fists, fear and rage rising inside her, fighting for dominance.

"As we move forward, stronger and more united, we must ensure that those within our walls remain loyal to the High Council's cause—our cause. Effective immediately, I hereby declare the permanent closure of St. Marrow's gates. No one will be permitted to enter or exit without undergoing full scanning and identification. Obey the Council."

Without hesitation, the crowd responds in unison, their voices mechanical, almost lifeless. "Survive the fog."

Violet's breath catches, the implication hitting her like a blow. The villagers, her people, are in more danger than ever.

Lucius was turning his sickening schemes to the vulnerable, the forgotten. The ones she swore to protect.

The camera zooms in on Lucius, exuding confidence as he stands before the roaring crowd—a wolf in sheep's clothing. He waves, basking in their frenzied cheers and shouts.

As the live feed cuts out, the tension in the room thickens, suffocating in its intensity. Each of them—Violet, Aiden, Ellie, Conrad and Elliot—are now unwilling players in the High Council's deadly mind games. Lucius has already marked them as dead, their scans erased by the decree. If they aren't careful, his lie will become their fate.

Aiden shakes his head, exchanging glances with Sophia. "Lucius doesn't know who he's up against," he says.

Violet nods, fire sparking in her gaze. "He will soon."

Acknowledgements

To my boyfriend, Mister William, my rock and constant support, thank you for always believing in me, motivating me, and helping me through every step of this writing and publishing journey.
I couldn't have done it without you.
To my younger brother, who has been my brainstorming partner and my very first beta reader, your insight and encouragement have been invaluable.
And to my sister, the incredibly talented artist behind this cover, thank you for bringing my vision to life with your creativity and skill.

About the Author

Tixa Carvalho crafts stories blending the paranormal,
dystopian worlds, and horror with world-ending stakes.
Born in north of Portugal, she shares her life with her
siblings and a handsome French-Canadian man.
Into the Paracosm is her debut dystopian horror book.
If you enjoy Tixa's books,
please don't forget to leave a review!

tiktok.com/@tixatheauthor
instagram.com/tixatheauthor

www.ingramcontent.com/pod-product-compliance
Lightning Source LLC
Chambersburg PA
CBHW030312160726
47992CB00005B/1977